Praise for *Last Song on Skye*

"Take an aging rocker who is Scotland's platinum blonde version of Elvis, his illegitimate child, some long standing resentments, and two American women trying to come to terms with their history. Put them all on the Isle of Skye, trailed by a reporter with no ethics or boundaries, but amusing as well as being annoying, and history will catch up with all of them. T.E. Swan has the gift of getting readers to care about her characters, whether they appear for just a few moments or travel from cover to cover. Her plot is skillfully written and riveting, and the narrative superbly paced. It's the kind of book where you can't wait to see what happens next."

  – Diane Frank, Author of *Mermaids and Musicians*

"What fun reading *Last Song on Skye*! This delightful debut mystery novel by T.E. Swan engages and entertains us with quirky characters and fast-paced whodunit mischief. Swan's two feisty protagonists lead us on a lively chase from San Francisco to London and finally to the Isle of Skye when their nostalgic visit to the past turns into a search to find a killer and clear themselves as murder suspects. Of course, we root for these indomitable women, but somehow, we can't quite hate the villains, thanks to Swan's writing skill. I suggest you add this book to your collection of cozy mysteries."

  – Elinor Gale, Author of *The Emancipation of Emily Rosenbloom*

Last Song on Skye

by
T. E. Swan

BLUE LIGHT PRESS ◆ 1ST WORLD PUBLISHING

SAN FRANCISCO ◆ FAIRFIELD ◆ DELHI

Last Song on Skye

1st World Library
PO Box 2211
Fairfield, IA 52556
www.1stworldpublishing.com

Blue Light Press
www.bluelightpress.com
bluelightpress@aol.com

Book & Cover Design
Melanie Gendron
melaniegendron999@gmail.com

Cover Art
Melanie Gendron

Author Photo
Harry A Haryanto
Harry Who Photography

First Edition

Library of Congress Cataloging-in-Publication Data

ISBN: 978-1-4218-3566-2

Acknowledgements

There are so many people to thank for helping me write this novel. I want to especially thank the OLLI Program at San Francisco State University for the many classes that allowed this retired civil servant to accomplish a long-held dream of writing mysteries about consumer safety problems I encountered while at the Consumer Product Safety Commission.

Special thanks goes to Diane Frank for her courses at OLLI, along with her private workshop. She kindly and gently guided me with her insistence on "Praise first" when reviewing everyone's work in group settings.

My classmate and talented editor, Elinor Gale, was invaluable. Thanks to many classmates in my writing groups and workshops for their feedback.

Thanks to the Mystery Writers workshop hosted by Book Passages, where I met some wonderful writers and gained some of their wisdom.

A great thanks goes to my dear friend, Barbara, whose travels with me over the years provided great ideas for the two women traveling in England and Scotland in my novel.

My dear friend and co-worker, Joel, (she/her) provided great ideas in our conversations about work investigations and our love of mysteries. She inspired ideas about the wise women in my novel.

Diane Frank and Bruce Herbold enhanced my descriptions of Scottish Country Dancing.

Many thanks to Calum MacKechnie, Director of OLLI Program at Dominican University, for sharing his memories of Skye and current slang in the UK.

Love and thanks to my daughter Stephanie, son Colin, and granddaughter Kaela for patient help with the mysteries of the internet and computers.

Last Song on Skye

New Beginnings

Phyllida sat in full lotus on her Princess Bukhara Persian carpet after completing her morning meditations. In early morning, her second-floor condominium overlooking Lafayette Park in San Francisco was sunny. The furnishings were simple, an ivory sofa and chairs. Her collection of paintings added color. Phyllida's favorite painting was a woman in a 1920s blue flapper dress in a Parisian bistro.

Recently widowed, Phyllida decided to leave her Santa Barbara senior living community. Since the death of her husband, Robert, she couldn't adjust to a life of golf and bridge. With a bit of urging from her long-time friend, Prudence Silver, she found a condo in San Francisco. Happily, this condo was two blocks from Prudence. Thirty-five years ago, Phyllida emigrated from London to San Francisco to marry Robert Walker, a cousin to Prudence Silver. She and Robert raised their only daughter, Beth, in the St. Francis Wood neighborhood of San Francisco. Now, she was adjusting to a new neighborhood in San Francisco across town from Beth.

She planned to invite Beth to lunch, but she was nervous about revealing travel plans she and Prudence were making. She was about to disclose an enormous secret she and Prudence had kept for more than 30 years.

Phyllida picked up her phone and dialed. "Hello, darling, I was wondering if I could have lunch with you today. I know it's short notice. Jaime will be there? What a treat! Lunch with my two favorite girls. How is Jaime adjusting to working at the martial arts studio? So happy to hear that, darling. Yes, that little restaurant near the Embarcadero would be perfect. Love to you and Jaime."

Luckily, Phyllida was on an electric bus line that took her directly to the Financial District. She was wearing a bright purple blouse, her favorite color, and black slacks with a black tweedy sweater.

Jaime looked out the window just as Phyllida was walking up the street. "Look, Beth. Your mother is so cute! A silver fox on the prowl for a wife might just snap her up."

"Lord, Jaime, I can't think of my mother dating. I'm still adjusting to my father being gone."

Beth and Jaime stood to hug Phyllida.

Phyllida, a petite white-haired woman, hugged Beth, a taller, brunette version of her mother, and Jaime, a light brown Afro-Asian woman. They ordered gourmet salads and indulged in warm sourdough bread dipped in herbed olive oil as they waited for their lunch.

"So, how are you two dear friends adjusting to not seeing each other daily?"

"Beth calls me in to do contract investigations and training almost weekly. Thank God she has Patrick McKay's old job as regional director." Jaime spoke animatedly.

"It seems that after Patrick McKay's death and the trial of Kirk Johnson, there's a completely new office staff with a lot of new people to train. I knew I trained Jaime well, and she's the perfect person for getting the newbies off to a professional start."

"Music to my ears! Consolidated Indemnity in San Francisco will set a marvelous example for the whole company. Ah, here's our lunch." The table fell silent as they each tasted their Crab Louie. The waiter expertly packaged their generous leftover salads to take home.

As they drank coffee, Phyllida shared her travel plans along with the old secret. "Well, darlings, Prudence and I are going to England to revisit our year of nursing study at Oxford. It will also retrace an old romance between Prudence and the singer, Amadeus."

"The Amadeus with long blond hair?" Jaime gasped, "Oh my God!"

"Yes, dears, the same. Prudence was the beauty among us, with long black hair and almond-shaped turquoise eyes. She and Amadeus traveled by motorcycle to nearby towns where

Amadeus and his group were performing. Near the end of the year, Prudence discovered she was pregnant. Amadeus disappeared as soon as she told him. We rushed her home to San Francisco where she reconnected with a long-time boyfriend, George Silver. Her parents supported a hasty marriage. The slightly premature baby, Vanessa, was born."

"Mother! You mean my cousin Vanessa is Amadeus' daughter? No wonder she has the platinum hair and the talent to become a ballerina! Lord, how much does Vanessa know?"

"Prudence waited a long time to tell Vanessa. Vanessa only learned the truth recently and is very angry with her mother. You probably shouldn't mention this to her just now."

"What made Prudence tell Vanessa now?" Beth sipped her coffee as she listened to her mother's story.

"Prudence has decided to get in touch with Amadeus to insist he acknowledge his daughter, Vanessa. When Prudence discovered she was pregnant, she also learned Amadeus had eloped with another girlfriend from his hometown on the Isle of Skye. These were very hard times for Prudence. That's why I came to San Francisco with her. It's also how I met your father, Robert, Prudence's cousin, at her wedding to George Silver."

"Gads, Mother, my head's spinning." Beth finished her coffee and handed money to the server before her mother could act.

"Why, thank you so much! I was planning on treating the two of you."

"We have to get back to the office, Mother. Keep me posted on your travel plans." Beth stood and hugged her mother. Jaime also hugged Phyllida before they left.

Travel Plans

Phyllida looked at her watch. "Time to meet with my favorite travel agent. Goodbye, darlings." She walked quickly to Love Travel, in Embarcadero Three.

She thought, *I think that went well. Pru's long-held secret is out and about to be more public if we visit Amadeus. Hope Linda at the travel agency can arrange comfortable accommodations in Portree, on the Isle of Skye.*

Phyllida took an escalator to the second floor of Embarcadero Three and entered the Love Travel Agency, tucked between a jeweler and a small dress shop. "Hi, I have an appointment with Linda." Phyllida spoke to a young man at the front counter.

"You certainly do, my dear!" Linda walked from her office with a happy smile. "My mother sends her best wishes."

"How is your mother? Is she fully recovered from her surgery?"

"Recovered and her energy is revved up. She's back working with her pre-school children. She's teaching them to tie their shoes. So important after nap time, you know."

"Wonderful to hear, Linda. Your mother announced the beginning of your travel agency several years ago. My travels have been much smoother since."

"You're my favorite client. I've worked up some ideas for England and Scotland you can review. I've been researching the Isle of Skye. Such a unique place where Vikings settled and mixed with the local population. What made you want to visit?"

"Oh, an old acquaintance used to speak poetically about his hometown on Skye."

"Really, do you plan to visit him? You'll get a more insider's view of the area."

"I'm not quite sure how that'll play out, but I'll see something unique either way."

"Great! There are some Viking festivals mentioned; be sure to get specifics from the locals while you're there. Sounds like some ancient rituals remain on the island."

Phyllida gathered all the brochures into a small tote. "Give my best to your mother. I'm so happy she's feeling better."

Phyllida phoned Prudence as soon as she arrived home. "Linda has some wonderful reservations lined up for us. Want to meet tomorrow at Starbucks to look them over? Yes, she has us at a bed & breakfast in Portree on the Isle of Skye near the end of our travels. I'm really looking forward to visiting our favorite places in London. I was planning on inviting some cousins to join us for high tea at the Queen Victoria Imperial Hotel if you don't mind. I can tell you're getting another call. See you at Starbucks tomorrow."

At 11:00 the next morning, Phyllida saw Prudence sitting at a window table in Starbucks. Prudence was still a beauty with straight silver hair cut into a short bob, framing her face with mesmerizing almond-shaped turquoise eyes. Prudence raised her cup as she saw her friend walking up the street.

Phyllida placed the travel brochures on the table as she stepped away to order her latte. Prudence was reading a brochure on Skye and the B&B in Portree as Phyllida returned to the table. She looked up at Phyllida. "I'm so grateful you're going to accompany me on this nostalgic journey."

"We've been close for so many years – the original trip to England started our friendship, your love affair with Amadeus, the baby, your marriage to George, and my meeting and marrying Robert. So, of course I'm with you all the way."

Prudence and Phyllida stared dreamily until Prudence's cell phone rang. "It's Vanessa. She's been in a snit since I told her about Amadeus. Better take this."

Laird of the Manor

Amadeus was near the end of his daily nine holes of golf at the Scotsmen's Private Club on Skye, 10 miles from Portree. "Bloody hell, Angus! I invite me brother for a couple of rounds, and now I lose and must buy the drinks! William, let the club know there will be three for single malt Skye whiskey and some of their famous mulligatawny soup in about 20 minutes."

William doffed his cap. "I'll get right on it, sir."

William, who had been driving the golf cart, handed the keys to the caddy and walked back to the clubhouse. The grey stone clubhouse, appearing as a stately old mansion with ivy growing up the walls was in reality built to the Skye Scotsmen's Private Club specifications just thirty years ago. Amadeus was a charter member.

After many glasses of whiskey with the hearty mulligatawny soup, Amadeus walked to his custom 2007 Rolls Royce, painted Queen Victoria blue. William and club employees did not dare question Amadeus' sobriety as he took the keys to drive to his estate five miles away. Muscle memory and a nearly deserted road contributed to arriving home without incident.

"William, get the demo CDs my fans and I have been reviewing for the coming grand tour this fall." Amadeus entered his luxurious old mansion and proceeded to his office.

Amadeus, a tall, heavyset man, still retained his handsome looks – that of a gracefully aging older man. His blond hair was dyed and held in a ponytail with a higher forehead than in his youth. As he sat at his large antique desk, he glanced at the day's mail. He picked up one thick envelope and gasped. *Why would she write after all this time?* With a vicious slit of the letter opener, he released the contents. "William, get me a glass of whiskey and bring the bottle." Amadeus read and reread the letter. He stared at the enclosed picture and printed reviews of the talented ballerina, Vanessa Silver.

William stepped into the office and found his boss asleep at his desk and gingerly removed the letter. He read it carefully and replaced the letter on the desk where Amadeus' wife, Florence, found and read it.

William walked in as she was reading. "I don't think Amadeus would want you to see this, Madam."

"I'm sure he would not want me to see this, but I knew there was another girl in Oxford that was up the spout when I discovered I was expecting our first-born, Llewellyn, our only daughter."

"So sorry you had to learn this way, Madam." William looked distressed as he spoke.

"Now, William, we both know what a philanderer my husband was in his earlier days." Florence carefully replaced the letter on the desk. "What a beautiful daughter! I'm sure her father will feel some pride, whether he deserves to or not."

Florence went to her own retreat: a combination office and sunroom. She pulled out the album of her early marriage with pictures of their four children. As she reminisced about her own children, she wondered about the early life of this beautiful, blond, American ballerina, the offspring of Amadeus' thirty-year-old indiscretion. Suspecting a child is so much easier than seeing it in the flesh. *Damn that man! But I am going to be the most beautiful, indulged, cuckolded wife in Scotland! Furthermore, my four children will take their proper places in society.*

Remembering a big dinner party by the MacQueens in Portree, Florence made appointments for hair and make-up. She would go even if Amadeus wasn't up to it.

She went to the sleeping Amadeus and gently woke him. "Love, I'm going to the beauty shop before the MacQueen party tonight. Are you coming? You seem a little tired."

"Absolutely, I'm attending! Must put in a word to keep the greedy county government out of me golf property. They want to erect a cell phone tower near our fourteenth hole, for God's sake! William, make sure me tartans are ready to wear tonight. Need to make an imposing figure of a true Scotsman."

Florence smiled to herself as she entered the back seat of the black Rolls Royce limo. She carried a garment bag and a small jewelry case.

That evening, Amadeus and Florence made an imposing grand entrance, photographed by a local reporter. Amadeus wore a McCloud plaid tartan. Florence sparkled in a black silk gown with sheer sleeves and flowing skirt. She carried a shawl of the MacDonald plaid. She wore several strands of gold chain interspersed with garnets, tourmalines, and amethysts. Matching earrings dangled almost to her shoulders. The pictures later posted in social media showed a gorgeous couple.

Amadeus badgered every local official, expressing his disapproval of the cell phone tower on the grounds of The Scotsmen's Private Club. During dinner, Amadeus' inebriated exuberance caused him to tip out of his chair, exposing boxers that didn't quite cover his manhood. Florence covered her mouth to hide her laughter as she watched two waiters straighten the chair and help Amadeus to a sitting position. A mug of strong coffee replaced the tumbler of scotch. Someone secretly took a photo of Amadeus in his full glory on the floor. This accompanied the MacQueen's posting of their glorious party on Facebook.

Halfway around the world in San Francisco, these pictures were viewed by Phyllida, Prudence, and Vanessa. In London, these pictures were viewed by Felicia Friday, a reporter for *London Daily Review*. She then looked up Amadeus on Facebook. There was an anonymous mention of the illegitimate daughter, Vanessa Silver, the American ballerina. In looking up Vanessa Silver's Facebook page, she saw the anonymous posting referring to Amadeus as the actual father of Ms. Silver. *I think I can get a great story with some research. Let me talk to my boss.*

Edinburgh, Scotland

Camilla Mackenzie finished her two hours as a radio presenter on Channel 2. She had an appointment with a reporter from *London Daily Review* for an interview regarding her singing days with Amadeus when they were all a small group on the Isle of Skye. She flagged a taxi and prayed that traffic would allow them to arrive on time.

The taxi driver was dazzled by this beautiful middle-aged woman with unnaturally bright red hair, a black fedora and a black leather jacket that didn't quite cover her buxom figure. Camilla wore stage make-up just in case pictures were taken.

"Can we make it to Café Ballater on Princes Street in 20 minutes? I have a generous tip if we do."

"Will try my best, madam." The young driver wore a plaid cap and spoke with a country Scottish accent.

Camilla dropped a 20 pound note. "Keep the change; you did your best." She ran the last two downhill blocks. Pausing to catch her breath, she regally entered the lobby of the historic old hotel.

"Pleased to see you, Ms. Mackenzie. Your pictures don't do you justice." Felicia Friday, a young blond reporter in a blue print Gloria Vanderbilt wrap dress, was standing at the entrance to direct Camilla to the side room furnished with a stationary camera and three chairs ready for the interview. "Your old singing partner, Johnny MacKay is already here."

Camilla hugged Johnny, a tall, thin, white-haired man in a pinstriped suit. "So long since we last met, Johnny. Hear good things of you in London."

"And I hear great things about you in Edinburgh. Hope we can get together for a drink after the interview."

Reporter Friday directed the two friends to the chairs to begin the interview. "If I understand correctly, you both sang with Amadeus when you were all very young."

"Actually, he was still Fergus MacCann. Johnny, Fergus, and I traveled to any event that would have us." Camilla spoke directly to the camera.

"Rumor has it you and Amadeus were more than friends, Ms. Mackenzie."

Johnny MacKay raised his hand. "Now steady on, Miss. We traveled and slept in the same housing and lodges, but there was nothing going on but music."

"Well, maybe I have it wrong. Was it you and Camilla having an affair?"

"I'm a poof, stupid woman!" Johnny and Camilla both huffed out of the interview.

Down the street, they sat at a pub drinking single malt scotch and catching up on old times. "Tell me why such a lovely woman as you never married, Camilla. We both know why I didn't."

"After the incident, there were complications that left me barren. It wasn't fair to marry a man when I couldn't give him his own child."

"Amadeus took better than he gave, the bastard!"

Among Friends and Family

Phyllida Walker was on the computer after her morning medita-tion and yoga. She had been following Amadeus on Facebook since she and her friend, Prudence, began planning their trip to England and Scotland's Isle of Skye. Thirty plus years ago, she and Prudence studied nursing at Oxford. Amadeus was singing regu-larly at Hare N' Hound, a popular student venue. Often, he sang directly to a lovely girl with long, black hair and turquoise eyes. Prudence stared lovingly back at him over her pint. One night, Prudence was invited backstage for conversation and cuddles with Amadeus. Within a few weeks, Prudence followed Amadeus to many concerts on the back of his Harley.

As her year of studies ended, so did her supply of birth con-trol pills. A few days' delay in arranging for birth control pills in England led to a night of unprotected passion. Her very regular monthly did not appear. This is how she found herself pregnant, and simultaneously, she learned that Amadeus had just eloped with a woman in his hometown of Portree, Skye.

After a whirlwind of soul searching and packing, Prudence returned to San Francisco with her friend and confidant, Phyllida. Of course, Prudence felt humiliated and angry. She quickly re-kindled an old romance. Luckily, a cousin invited the family to her grand wedding. George Silver was Prudence's escort. They danced under an arbor of wisteria and jasmine as their love bloomed into a romance. They had been dear friends since 7th grade.

Amadeus had given Prudence money for a termination, which she used toward the wedding. Prudence and George opted for a small wedding ceremony at San Francisco City Hall followed by a wonderful family party at the Fairmont Hotel. Vanessa Silver arrived slightly premature. As a happy coincidence, at the wed-ding, Phyllida met and soon married Prudence's cousin, Robert Walker.

Prudence and George enjoyed a happy marriage. They socialized within their country club, and George became wealthy as an investment banker. They lived near Phyllida and Robert in San Francisco.

A year later, Prudence's husband, George Silver, passed away after 31 years of marriage. Three months ago, Prudence invited Vanessa for lunch at her home and reluctantly told her the truth about her biological father. Vanessa was furious. "Mother, how could you keep this a secret from me for so long? This affects my husband and my two children, not just me."

"Well, darling, you and your dad had such a special relationship I just couldn't spoil it. Your dad, George, would have been so devastated if he had known."

Vanessa Silver, a principal ballerina with the San Francisco Ballet, was known for her trademark platinum hair, which was Amadeus' trademark feature as well. Yuri Chermovsky, Vanessa's husband, was also a principal dancer at the Ballet. Vanessa was returning to her best professional level after giving birth to two children – Ivan, now a three-year-old, and Dimitry, a two-year-old.

Vanessa was reluctant to tell Yuri about the famous Scottish singer being her father. Yuri was very old-fashioned about illegitimacy. Along with this, Yuri's Russian family had been reluctant for him to marry a convert to Judaism from outside the Russian culture.

Vanessa began following Amadeus on Facebook. Today, she'd seen a wonderful picture of Amadeus with his beautiful wife at a gathering in Scotland. Further down the entry was an anonymous post showing Amadeus sprawled on the floor, obviously drunk with his kilt askew. Still further below was another anonymous post. "This must be quite the embarrassment to his illegitimate daughter, the lovely ballerina, Vanessa Silver."

Vanessa gasped as she saw the post, outing her as the bastard daughter of Amadeus.

Damn you, Mother, for keeping this secret! Yuri will be shaken, and my Russian princess mother-in-law will be horrified. I adored

my dad, George Silver. I even became Jewish to worship with him.
Who the hell is putting these snide remarks on Amadeus' page?

Phyllida knew that Prudence didn't follow Facebook, so she invited her over for tea and conversation. Luckily, Prudence lived only two blocks away – an enjoyable walk through Lafayette Park. She could smell the fresh baked scones as she knocked on the door.

"Come on in, Pru. Let me get you a cup of tea. Earl Grey okay?" Being English, Phyllida had made a proper pot of tea. They sat at the round dining table with Wedgewood plates, cups and warm scones, farmers' market strawberry jam, and clotted cream.

"Philly, you spoil me. No wonder I like you so much." Prudence stirred her tea with milk and sugar and devoured the scone with jam and cream. "When you called, you said there was something you needed to show me."

"We're going to look first at Amadeus' Facebook page, then at Vanessa's page. Some anonymous person is posting entries outing Amadeus as Vanessa's biological father."

"Oh Lord! Who's doing that?" Prudence buried her face in her hands. "Vanessa is going to be livid."

Phyllida gave her friend a hug. "I'm in your corner all the way. Today's morality is so much more relaxed than when Vanessa was conceived. You were just ahead of your time."

"True, but Vanessa has old-fashioned Russian in-laws who see her as an outsider because she grew up outside the Russian culture and became Jewish by conversion."

Vanessa's Dilemma

Vanessa was watching *Sesame Street* with her children. Dimitry looked up as she was wiping away tears.

"Why crying, Mommy?" Dimitry hugged his mother's legs and looked up with his beautiful blue eyes.

"Mommy just felt sad for a minute, baby."

"Ivan and me are good boys, Mommy."

Vanessa sank gracefully to her heels and hugged both boys. "You are my true happiness."

"Ok, Mommy."

The grind of the garage door announced Yuri's return from the gym.

"Hi, Daddy!" The boys ran for the back stairs just as Yuri emerged with a red rose for his wife.

"Mommy is sad," announced Dimitry.

Ivan reached to hug Vanessa's knees again. "I love Mommy."

"What's the matter, Lubchik?" Yuri turned to Vanessa and gave her a hug.

"Better sit down, luv. It's a long story." Vanessa was holding Dimitry as she spoke. "Are you familiar with the Scottish singer, Amadeus?"

"Of course, my mother is a great fan. She has all his albums."

"Amadeus and my mother had a fling when she was studying in England."

Yuri sat down. "Really. Oh my God! Your blonde hair! Did your dad, George Silver, know?"

"No one knew but Aunty Phyllida. I'm just furious with Mother for keeping this secret then dumping it on me now!" Vanessa pounded her fist on the kitchen counter.

Yuri moved Dimitry to the floor then took Vanessa into his arms with a big hug that became a twirl around the room. Vanessa's frown turned to a smile with the twirling. "I'm relieved that

I could tell you about it, luv. What do you think your mother's reaction will be?"

"There's no hurry to tell my family. We can take our time. Speaking of time, we need to get ready for the children's check-ups. Can you believe day cares require doctors' certificates and updates on vaccinations?" Yuri grumbled. "Ok, boys, let me clean your faces and hands." Yuri had a wet wipe in hand as each boy tried to avoid the cleanup. "Want me to come along to lend a hand, Lubchik?"

"Sure. Make sure Dimitry has his Binky and blanket square. I don't want a meltdown if we can avoid it."

"Come on boys, I'll put you in your car seats." Yuri led the children down the stairs into the open garage.

When they parked by the doctor's building, Ivan began crying. "No shots!" he screamed. Dimitry's eyes widened in fear, and he was about to cry as well.

"Come on, Ivan, this is just a check-up. No shots today." Vanessa hugged Ivan as she helped him out of his seat.

Yuri picked up Dimitry. They walked into the pediatrician's office, furnished with soft cubes in bright colors for the children. Dimitry and Ivan soon began tumbling around the carpet.

Dr. Yang was a dedicated pediatrician as well as a big fan of the SF Ballet. He usually looked forward to talking with Vanessa and Yuri, but not today. "I'm so glad both of you came today. I have some news that may be nothing or could be very serious." Dr. Yang directed his assistant to watch the children as he led the parents to his office. "Dimitry shows signs of a unique anemia, which may be a sign of early leukemia. I'll need further tests at UCSF Hospital to make an accurate determination. Are there any family members with an unusual type of anemia? This is common among Nordic ethnicities."

Vanessa felt her stomach clench. "I'm not sure. Do I have time to investigate? My father is Scottish, but I know very little about him. My mother is English and French."

"I'm pretty much Russian Jew," Yuri said. "Probably some Slavic. When do we need the answer?"

"The blood test and a DNA check will answer the question. We'll draw blood from each of you at the hospital. My assistant will make an appointment."

Yuri and Vanessa led the children to their car. "Time for waffles at IHOP!" cheered Ivan.

"I love waffles!" Dimitry shouted through his Binky.

"Boy, do I have words for Mother! I don't even know my heritage!" Vanessa hissed to Yuri.

"To be fair, both of your parents are to blame. Wonder if Amadeus is Nordic? I've read that Vikings settled in northern Scotland. Some Vikings settled along the Volga as well. Maybe I'm Nordic."

"I hope our baby doesn't have leukemia!" Vanessa began crying.

"Let's not panic until we know the full story. We need to put on a brave face for our children!"

News – Not All Good

Prudence eyed the fresh clams on sale at Mollie Stone's. Clams with garlic and wine was one of her specialties. She dialed Phyllida. "Hi, Philly, are you free for dinner at my place? Mollie Stone's has fresh clams."

"I sure am. What a treat! Our usual time, about 6? I'll chill a bottle of good Chardonnay I've been saving."

Just as Prudence finished talking with Phyllida, the phone rang. She recognized the name of her financial advisor. George Silver had left many investments, including a trust for her.

"Mrs. Silver, have you seen today's news? The stock market has crashed. Unfortunately, some of your investments have lost value."

"Oh Lord!" Prudence sat heavily on a chair. "Am I ruined? I thought steps had been taken to prevent such a fall after the Lincoln Savings and Loan mess a few years ago."

"No, you're not ruined, but the trust value has dropped 20%. Don't withdraw anything from this trust until things settle. As you know, the market cycles up and down. Your investments may regain value."

"I'm going to have to sit and digest this news. I'll call you back with my questions."

Prudence sat in silence for an hour before calling Phyllida. "Change of plans, friend. I'm ordering pizza for dinner, and I need your good company. My broker just called to say my trust has dropped 20% in value."

"I'll bring red wine and we'll talk. I'm so sorry this happened. I remember your George being so careful to see that you were well provided for."

Phyllida pulled a Merlot off the wine rack and put on her jacket. As she walked across Lafayette Park, she wondered if their trip to England and Scotland was still on.

At 6:00, Prudence saw Phyllida walking up to her house and opened the door. "Come on into the kitchen. We'll open the wine right now if you don't mind."

Phyllida struggled with the corkscrew and poured the elixir into beautiful Waterford glasses.

"In case you're wondering, I still have enough money for our trip."

"I was wondering. You know we could postpone the trip for a later time."

"No, I don't want to do that. I have other sources of money, and the arrangements we've made seem right to me." Just then the doorbell rang. "That'll be pizza from Dino's."

In silence, the women ate slices of vegetarian with eggplant pizza served on red paper plates.

"Vanessa called me yesterday with health news about Dimitry. The doctor says that he has an odd form of anemia that might be precursor to leukemia. It seems this is a common form of anemia among Nordic races. Could Amadeus be Nordic?"

"Oh my God! That's frightening! I certainly hope it's not leukemia. It's quite possible Amadeus is Nordic. Our travel agent read up on Skye. It seems that there are some ancient Nordic rituals continuing from the Viking invasions. Evidently, Vikings remained in the highlands and mixed with the Scots."

"I'll have to tell Vanessa right away. I think I'll text. She's so difficult to talk to these days."

Happy Birthday, Amadeus

Amadeus was fifth in a family of eight. As a child, when his birthday came, presents were not affordable. They celebrated with a cake for dinner with the family gathered around the piano to sing afterwards. As an affluent adult, Amadeus always had extravagant birthday parties. He and Florence would pretend that she had forgotten about his birthday as she planned the great surprise. This year was no exception. Florence had arranged for a geodesic dome to be constructed near the swimming pool and had sent invitations to friends and family.

On his birthday, Amadeus went to the Gentlemen's Club of Skye, where he was a founding member. In the early afternoon, he golfed, played billiards, and returned home with his brother, Angus, and his personal assistant, William. Florence was in the front garden with her clippers and basket, deadheading some old blooms. Under her gardening jacket, she was wearing a black, sequined shirt with an elaborate necklace of large hematite stones and a jade dragon in the center.

As the blue Rolls Royce pulled into the drive, Florence was clipping a rose bush. "You're gardening late, Lass!" Amadeus exited the passenger side.

"Thought I'd get the rose bush ready for spring. Could you and the lads carry these cans down to the compost pile?"

As the three men and Florence walked down the sloping yard, the geodesic dome near the pool became visible. "What's that?" muttered Amadeus.

"Let's walk over and see," suggested Florence as she led the way.

Everyone in the geodesic dome, friends and family, was totally silent until Amadeus approached the front. Suddenly a band began to play "Happy, Happy Birthday Baby" with all the guests loudly singing.

"You really fooled me this time, Lass!" Amadeus gave Florence a hug and kiss before joining the party.

The decor included a life-sized cutout of Amadeus with his arm pointed to tables of food and drink. At one giant table, waiters were ready to carve a large prime rib and a leg of lamb. In front of the meats were small roasted potatoes, carrots, parsnips, and pearl onions. Another table presented a large smoked salmon, surrounded with spiced and boiled langoustine, lightly sautéed spinach, kale, broccoli, marinated mushrooms, olives, and artichoke hearts. The band nestled close to the food, across from tables flowing with beer, wine, whiskey, and champagne.

Amadeus joined a group near the drinks table to talk and have pictures taken. He grasped the women tightly around the waist for the photographs, especially the young women. Callum MacQueen, the photographer from the *Skye Sentinel,* was walking around taking candid photos. Callum was a classmate of Amadeus' oldest son, Fergus. In fact, Callum had dated Fiona before she married Fergus. Fergus suspected that Callum knew Fiona in the biblical sense, although Fiona denied it. Callum left while the party was still in full revelry to get his pictures to the *Sentinel* in time for tomorrow's society page.

As Callum drove the narrow country road towards Portree, he was run into a ditch by a car with its high beams on. As he exited his car on uneven ground, he was blinded by the bright lights. He remembered nothing after a heavy hit to the head.

The following morning, Amadeus, his children, and relatives from the party were having a morning brunch on the terrace just off the dining room. Sean McDermott, Chief Editor of the *Skye Sentinel,* and an old schoolmate of Amadeus, came by to inquire about his photographer, Callum MacQueen, who seemed to have disappeared, with his car abandoned on the side of the road.

"Welcome Sean! Have a seat and join us." Amadeus waved to an empty chair.

"Would do, Amadeus, but I've a missing photographer and reporter. Callum never showed up last night at the *Sentinel.*

His car was found abandoned on the side of the road today. The pictures from your party were sent in, though. Looks like a great celebration."

After Sean left, Amadeus looked over at Florence. "Did you approve any pictures for the paper?"

"No, I didn't approve anything, Love."

Family DNA

Prudence had agreed to accompany her daughter and son-in-law with Dimitry on their trip to the doctor's for follow-up tests. Vanessa often called on her because of her nursing skills. She stood on her front porch, listening to a nest of robins singing as she waited for the blue Prius. She entered the backseat next to Dimitry in his car seat.

"No doctor! No shot!" shouted Dimitry, as Prudence took his hand.

"Darling, I don't think there will be any shots, but if there are you have my permission to scream as loud as you please." Prudence patted his chubby hand.

Vanessa turned and glared from the front seat. Prudence smiled back sweetly. Yuri knew he had to resist laughing or Vanessa would explode.

The physician's assistant ushered everyone into a small examining room to take DNA swabs. Prudence pulled a Cara Black mystery from her tote and read for the ten minute wait. Dimitry ran to her knees and looked up, "No shots, Gran. Do we go for ice cream or IHOP?"

"Which would you prefer, darling?"

"Ice cream!"

"Well, let's go to Mitchell's then."

Yuri and Vanessa needed some levity to replace fears for their son's health. Going for ice cream sounded wonderful.

Three weeks later, the test results showed Vanessa was 65% British, 25% Scottish and 10% Scandinavian. Surprisingly, Yuri's results showed 70% Ashkenazi Jewish, 20% Slavic Russian and 10% Scandinavian. Dimitry came by his Scandinavian traits from both parents. Yuri begged Vanessa not to reveal these results to his Russian Jewish mother.

A personal phone call from the doctor assured Yuri and Vanessa that Dimitry did not have leukemia. The anemia he had routinely appeared in the Scandinavian ethnic groups. The doctor prescribed vitamins with iron taken daily with a follow up blood test in six months.

When Prudence heard the results, she was very relieved. She'd warned Phyllida she'd have to cancel the trip if Dimitry was diagnosed with cancer. She now called Phyllida to assure her the trip was back on.

"Hooray," shouted Phyllida as she heard the good news. Prudence took the phone away from her ear. "Let's decide what to pack. I want everything in one 26-inch roll on. How about you?"

"Well, Philly, I tend to overpack, but this sounds great. I'll work with you to travel light for a change."

Expect the Unexpected

Beth called her mother with a wonderful invitation. "Hi, Mom, the twins are coming home for breaks before summer school. I thought I could fire up the grill for chicken and your great bar-beque sauce."

"Marvelous, darling. When and what time?"

"This evening around 6. Sorry for the late notice."

"I'll be there. Want me to make a shrimp salad?"

"Wonderful, I have some corn on the cob to grill. We'll have a feast."

Phyllida smiled to herself, remembering all the cookouts she, Beth, and Robert had enjoyed in the past. She put on her jacket and walked to Mollie Stone's for shrimp. At 5 p.m., she gently combined macaroni, shrimp, finely chopped Maui onion, finely chopped dill pickle, and her favorite mayonnaise. She reserved a small amount for herself and lidded the large bowl. With her big bag, she walked to her car parked in Prudence's garage. As Phyllida shopped for a condominium, Prudence had urged her to buy the condo only two blocks away, but it didn't have a garage. Phyllida agreed to purchase the condo with the promise that she could park her car in Prudence's two-car garage.

The cookout and visit with Beth and the children was in the small backyard with everyone sitting at a wood picnic table, sharing food and plans for school and Phyllida's coming trip with Prudence. They just relaxed, ate, and talked. The twins were so enthused about their classes at Stanford. Alex, starting a mustache, was studying engineering with interest in computers and robots. Kate, a raven-haired beauty like her mother, was studying political science and hoped to get into law school. At 9:30, Phyllida helped with the cleanup and then drove home. It was late and she didn't want to disturb Prudence, so she put her car in the garage and began walking through Lafayette Park to her condo. The park looked deserted. She had agreed to call an Uber whenever it was dark, but this time, she decided not to bother her friend.

Suddenly, three young men with long hair and tattoos emerged from the nearby trees. One of them grabbed her purse. Phyllida held onto her purse and screamed. She fell to the ground and hit her head on a rock as her purse was wrenched away. Just as suddenly, Prudence was running into Lafayette Park in house slippers and waving an iron skillet. A police car drove into the park's service road as the young men scattered. Phyllida's grocery bag with the chicken and bowl was lying in the grass. Over Phyllida's objections, she was taken by ambulance to the nearest emergency room. Prudence rode along with her. Phyllida begged, "Prudence, don't call Beth. She doesn't need to be worried."

"Too late, friend. She and the twins are in the lobby waiting to see you."

"Gads! Do I look as bad as I feel?"

"Not bad for a woman just mugged in the park. I thought we agreed that you would put your car in the garage, come into the house, and call an Uber."

"I didn't want to disturb you. The lights were off. I thought you were asleep."

"Well, I was disturbed, all right. The police are taking me home. You can visit with Beth and the kids. You're spending the night."

Beth Rand arrived at the Emergency Room in a long trench coat over the flannel leopard pants she used as pajamas. The twins were in jeans and sweatshirts. Prudence came from the small ER patient room. She directed the family in to see Phyllida. Beth was in tears. She rushed into the room with the twins right behind. Phyllida had a swollen black eye, and the right side of her face was swollen and badly bruised.

"Mother! This is awful! From now on, I'm picking you up and taking you home!"

"I look worse than I feel, darlings. Maybe I should take that self-defense class Jaime is always talking about."

"Great idea, Gran." Alex and Kate chimed in together.

Lessons Learned

The next morning, Phyllida came home from the hospital with Beth and the twins hovering like well-intentioned bees. She was bruised and battered with a black eye and bruises from forehead to chin on the right side of her face. She went straight to bed. With pillows propped, she read the paper and watched television. The twins brought fresh pots of tea to her bedside, followed by minestrone with toasted sourdough bread. Prudence promised to bring dinner, as Beth had to return to work, and the twins were heading back to school. Phyllida was grateful for the peace and quiet to nap. She was exhausted, feeling aches and pains all over her body.

At 5p.m., Prudence arrived with a dinner and a stack of her favorite mysteries Phyllida hadn't read. The women sat at the kitchen table to eat a fresh salad of romaine, tomatoes, and avocado. The main course was Prudence's special turkey meatloaf with hot and sweet mustard topping and sautéed mushrooms with sherry and creme fraiche.

"Pru dear, you're an amazing cook. This is wonderful." Phyllida squeezed a little more of the hot and sweet mustard onto the meatloaf.

"It's hard to cook for one. Keep the leftovers."

"That's fine with me. I don't cook much anymore, either."

"Now onto more serious things. We're going to England in eight weeks. I just found a two week self-defense for women class starting next week. Will you be well enough to take it with me?"

"I may not look my best, but I'm more than ready to learn some self-defense. Those thugs need to get clobbered by a woman who knows how to defend herself! By the way, the police found my purse and ID minus the money."

"That's wonderful! Did you identify the three men yet?"

"I picked them out of a photo line-up while in the hospital.

They're in a gang known to law enforcement, but they haven't been apprehended."

"Friends of Lafayette Park are now patrolling with big dogs from sundown until 10 p.m. Our neighbors are alarmed by your assault."

"Well, Pru, there's something positive coming from this awful experience."

The following week, the two women were standing barefoot on well-worn mats, learning power screams and power moves with five other women. At the beginning of each session, the women sat on their mats to discuss ways to look and behave more aggressively and appear less vulnerable. Everyone was given pepper spray on the first day. When the two-week session ended, Prudence and Phyllida celebrated by going to a favorite high tea at Lovejoy's in the Mission.

"This should prepare us for the Queen Victoria high tea in London. We had such good times there as young women." Phyllida bit into a cream cheese and cucumber sandwich.

"We certainly did. I hope we can get discount tickets to a play from Leicester Square. Half the fun is the trip to Leicester Square and the discount." Prudence took a bite of her scone with strawberry jam.

"How's your packing coming along?" Phyllida raised an eyebrow as she looked at Prudence.

"What, you've already started packing? Won't everything get wrinkled?"

"I put a portable dress rack in my spare bedroom and use the guest bed to lay out what I intend to take. This keeps me from overdoing it at the last minute."

"That's a wonderful idea. I'll start tomorrow."

"Tomorrow, I'm visiting Sister Mary John at Mercy Center to get back into meditation. I'll be happy to share meditations with you on the trip."

"That's right, you were really into meditation and centering prayer when you were younger. Meditation has become really trendy since then, hasn't it? Oprah has many guests on her show who are into self-help and metaphysical pursuits. I love Deepak Chopra."

"I stopped doing meditation for several years until Beth and Jaime were dealing with being prime suspects for murder. Now, my meditation has been spotty. After my mugging, I know I need to reconnect."

Sister Mary John at Mercy Center

When Phyllida phoned Sister Mary John, the nun invited her to lunch. "Our food is from the garden we cultivate as part of our spiritual practice, and after lunch we can spend the rest of the afternoon catching up and meditating."

"Oh, Mary J, that would be just like the early days! I really need your insight and wisdom."

Two days later, Phyllida went from a gray San Francisco morning into sunlight as she drove south on Highway 280 to Burlingame. As she entered Mercy Center grounds, she admired the blooming azaleas and rhododendrons. When she walked into the Visitor's Center, Sister Mary John was talking with the receptionist as she awaited her guest.

"Phyllida, such a pleasure to see you. But wait a minute, your face is bruised. What happened?"

"Long story short, I was mugged in Lafayette Park."

Sister Mary John took Phyllida's shoulders and turned her to the light for a better look. "How awful! Hope your spiritual and physical injuries mend quickly. Come, tell me more over lunch. The sisters' garden makes a wonderful buffet. I just love the summer vegetables."

Phyllida heaped her plate with fresh lettuces, tomatoes, cucumbers, zucchini, and summer squashes, home-cured pickles with a variety of sliced cheeses and slices of homemade bread. Then, Sister Mary John led them to a small table to eat and talk.

"Philly, we seem to get together when you're in crisis. Last year, your daughter was accused of murder and now you were mugged." Sister Mary John poured them each a glass of fresh lemonade as she spoke. The nun was a small woman with graying brown hair and clear brown eyes. She wore brown slacks, a beige sweater, and a wooden cross on a leather strap. Her face had a calmness that exuded trust.

"After my husband died and I moved back to San Francisco, I've veered from one crisis to another. My best friend, Prudence, is going through it too. She's about to seek out an old lover living in Scotland, the father of her oldest child."

"This makes me very thankful I reserved the entire afternoon. We'll talk about all of this. I hope you know you're more than welcome to continue working with me weekly, just as we did in the old days. I lead a group you'd be very compatible with on Wednesday afternoons. I think a person gets great insight by hearing other people's dilemmas. Everything shared in these groups is totally private. Everyone is conscientious about preserving anonymity."

"I'm very thankful for your insight and wisdom, Mary J."

Sister Mary John led Phyllida to a cozy room decorated with photographs and artwork, showing women from around the world carrying baskets on their heads, gardening, milking goats, weaving wool, and tending the sick. Phyllida chose an armchair, and Mary John pulled her chair to sit across from her, their knees almost touching.

"I believe you and your friend, Prudence, are very fortunate to have each other's support as you adjust to empty nests and widowhood. The trip you two are planning has the potential of healing youthful impetuousness, but there may be long held anger and resentments stirred up as well. The two of you may face unexpected complications."

Phyllida felt herself shudder slightly. "Pru and I will be very careful not to intrude into Amadeus' life if he's unwilling to meet with us. Pru wants him to acknowledge his daughter and appreciate that she was well brought up. That sounds perfectly reasonable to me."

"Yes, it is reasonable; however, Amadeus and his family may not want to admit his paternity. Prudence and her daughter should be prepared to be ignored or outright rejected."

"You're right. We should prepare for the unexpected."

"Now let's meditate. Sit back comfortably with your feet on the floor and your eyes gently closed. Take several deep breaths and relax into a natural rhythm of breath. Feel the room filling with a gentle light. Feel your body merge with the light as you walk along a gentle path. As your path becomes steep and rocky, the light becomes your strength. As the path becomes gentle, the light becomes soft and gentle.

"The light guides you to a safe, warm cave lined with Persian rugs and soft pillows, where you can sit and rest safely. The light is your guide and your strength. It becomes bright and gentle as needed. Call on the light for your insight and safety. The light is always with you. Now, rest for a few minutes breathing in the light of safety."

After 20 minutes of silence, Sister Mary John spoke softly. "As you gradually return, you have the light with you always. You can ask and the light will be your strength. Now, open your eyes."

Phyllida opened her eyes. Her body felt light and refreshed. The tension she was unaware of had lifted. Mary J. gave her a hug, then walked with her to the front entrance. Phyllida drove home in a state of euphoria. She was glad to park her car in Prudence's garage and go upstairs to share this wonderful experience with her friend.

Travel Time

Excitement and anxiety surged through the travelers as they put their dreams in motion. Vanessa drove her mother and Phyllida to the International Terminal of SFO. They had reservations on British Air for an afternoon departure direct to London. The women were three hours early in case of problems and each was armed with a book.

"Phyllida, how clever you were to wear those clogs. Getting through security was so much easier than with my lace-up sneakers."

"I love my purple clogs." Phyllida was dressed in black denim pants with a purple blouse and a tweedy black sweater, comfortable for travel.

Prudence looked lovely as usual in a blue denim pant suit and white silk shirt. "I can't believe we're going back to England. We had such good times as students."

"But keep in mind, we're different from the girls we were then."

"Of course."

The women took their time along the long walkways to browse high end perfume, books, magazines, and snacks for their long flight. They finally settled into their chairs in the boarding area with Starbucks lattes.

They quietly read until it was time to board. They had chosen an aisle seat for Phyllida and window seat for Prudence in the same row. The person in the middle offered to change seats, but they declined.

They tried to rest, despite three children seated behind them kicking a steady tattoo on the back of their seats. Small arms shot between the seats at unexpected times. Glares from Phyllida and Prudence caused temporary respite, while their parents across the aisle were oblivious.

Moving through British Customs was slow for Prudence.

Phyllida entered with her British passport and waited for Prudence in baggage claim. By the time Prudence arrived, Phyllida had both their checked bags on a luggage cart. They exited and quickly spotted the sign for their hotel limo. They tried not to sleep for the hour's drive; however, they broke travel rules and took a four-hour nap in their room. Awake and still somewhat drowsy, they decided to explore their neighborhood.

"Oh look, Philly, there's a Boots just next door. Let's do a quick browse. I need something for my sinuses. The airplane's dry air left me with a burning nose."

"I see a Tesco's at the far corner. Let's find some snacks for our room."

Prudence consulted with a pharmacist – chemist by British terms – and made her purchase. They passed a children's clothing shop. The child mannequins were holding British flags as they exhibited the current trend in British school clothes.

"Look at these English schoolboy outfits. I'll have to get something like this for my grandsons."

The women walked leisurely down the block to Tesco's to look for snacks and possibly a picnic box for the train.

"Hooray, a small jar of Marmite! I haven't had any in years." Phyllida clutched the small jar of the beer yeast derivative the Brits loved.

"All yours, Philly. I think it must be an acquired taste. I can't stand the stuff."

Prudence continued down the aisle to the cheese section and picked up a small package of Stilton, with its stripes of blue cheese. "This will be wonderful on crackers."

The women continued to walk and enjoy London's sights and sounds with double decker buses and big black taxis interspersed with delivery trucks driving along the left side of the roadway.

"You know, Pru, I'm getting a bit peckish. Why don't we return to the hotel and see if the bar has pub food?"

"Great! I hope they have the television turned to the evening news. I love hearing about local happenings. I'm hungry as well. I might just have a shandy for old time's sake."

The bar was lined with small wooden tables and benches against the wall. As the two sat down, the barman approached the table with menus and a request for drink orders. Phyllida ordered a half pint of light ale, and Prudence ordered a shandy. They chose a platter with a variety of cheeses, chutney, and brown bread – the Ploughman's Platter. The barman agreed to include a few carrot and celery sticks at no charge.

The television was on the evening news. Everyone in the pub was watching an episode called "Where Are They Now?" Felicia Friday appeared and presented her interview with Camilla Mackenzie and Johnny MacKay, former singers with Amadeus. The interview showed Mackenzie and MacKay storming off with MacKay's exclamation, "I'm a poof, you idiot!" Felicia Friday spoke afterwards and emphasized Amadeus' reputation for womanizing. She suggested that Mackenzie might have been one of Amadeus' conquests.

An older man with his wife at another table commented, "That bloke sure had the lasses lined up in his day!" Prudence could feel her face reddening as she fought back the tears.

Phyllida grabbed the barman's sleeve as he passed, "Sir, could we get this food packed to take to our rooms?"

Prudence whispered, "Thank you," as they gathered the packages and headed for the elevator. "I'm such a ninny. Maybe this was all a bad idea, Philly."

"Nonsense! We came here to have a great vacation in England. Tomorrow, we go to Leicester Square to see about theatre tickets, and the day after we're having high tea. Remember, we're meeting some of my cousins. I don't know if you remember Betty. She visited us at Oxford the year we were studying. We don't have to find Amadeus if you don't want to. We can change plans for the rest of the trip. We're free to decide day by day."

"You're such a wonderful friend. I can really trust you."

Leicester Square and High Tea

They rode the Underground to Leicester Square, an adventure that brought back memories from thirty years ago. They lunched in a small restaurant specializing in jacket potatoes, sharing a broccoli and cheddar potato. Then on to the discount box office to choose theatre tickets. To their surprise, a billboard featured an Amadeus concert tour at the Palladium in two days. Prudence couldn't stop staring at the picture of an older Amadeus in his full tartans.

"Philly, do you think we could get tickets in the balcony? We would be totally inconspicuous. I'd love to hear him sing again."

"I'll support whatever you want, Pru," but Phyllida felt a misgiving as she spoke.

After buying tickets, the women boarded a hop on and off London sightseeing bus. They hopped off at Trafalgar Square to watch a falcon soaring and returning to his falconer. Apparently, the sight of the falcon soaring was enough to discourage pigeons without the falcon consuming any of them. They hopped back on the sightseeing bus, headed for the Tower of London and joined a yeoman's tour that included viewing the crown jewels. The Victoria Bridge – painted Queen Victoria's favorite blue – invited them to walk across the Thames on this sunny day.

"Let's walk across the bridge and catch the Tube for home. I see the station on this map," Prudence said, pointing to her pocket map.

The walk across the bridge was six blocks farther than they realized. As they exited the Marble Arch near their hotel, their feet demanded rest. They purchased Indian take-out and ate in their room with their feet propped up.

The following day, Phyllida and Prudence looked elegant as they left for high tea. Phyllida wore a black pantsuit with a floral purple blouse. Prudence wore a navy pantsuit with a pastel

Liberty of London camisole in shades of blue and turquoise. They arrived a few minutes early to meet Phyllida's cousin, Betty, and her daughter, Lisa.

Unknown to the two women, Vanessa had posted best wishes to her mother for this nostalgic high tea on her Facebook page. Felicia Friday had been surreptitiously following Amadeus and Vanessa Silver's Facebook pages after the mention of her relationship to Amadeus. She had been seriously chastised for her interview of Camilla Mackenzie and Johnny MacKay. Now, she hoped to redeem herself by getting some information on Prudence, who really did have an affair with Amadeus. She made reservations for the Queen Victoria High Tea. Felicia had recently been diagnosed with type II diabetes, but she was still in denial of the need to change her diet. Thus, she chose Champagne, chocolate strawberries, and custard tarts from the extensive menu.

She was on her second glass of Champagne when she observed the four women being seated across the room. She had studied Vanessa's Facebook page and found a picture of Prudence holding her grandson. She recognized the woman in the navy suit as Prudence, but she was frustrated not to be able to hear their conversation. She photographed them with her phone while pretending to photograph the stained-glass skylight. During her third glass of Champagne, Felicia fainted and fell out of her chair.

The waiter rushed over and loudly called, "Is there a doctor or nurse in the room?"

Prudence and Phyllida, both nurses, looked around and came to Felicia's assistance. The blonde thirty-something woman, who lay semi-conscious and flushed, began to wake and attempted to get up.

"Don't try to sit up just yet, dear," Phyllida ordered.

"She's flushed and her pulse is shallow," Prudence said, after checking her pulse and looking into her eyes. "She needs emergency assistance."

Just as they spoke, a paramedic with a portable rolling chair arrived and checked Felicia's pulse and blood pressure. "Do you have any medical conditions we should know about, Miss?"

"I might have a little diabetes," Felicia meekly admitted.

"What! You were having Champagne and sweets! Very poor choices." The indignant paramedic wheeled Felicia to an ambulance as Phyllida and Prudence rose from the floor and dusted off their pant legs.

"That woman sure looks familiar," Prudence muttered as she returned to her table.

"That woman is the television presenter who hosts the *Where Are They Now* series," Betty observed. You probably saw her on television."

"Poor woman," Phyllida stated. "Now let's choose a tea. Earl Grey okay with everyone? I see a wonderful selection of sandwiches and scones with clotted cream."

Amadeus at the Palladium

Amadeus arrived at the Palladium a day before the show to rehearse and do sound checks. A crew had prepared the dressing room with flowers, champagne, and small sandwiches. As they rehearsed, a worker in a blue jumpsuit spent a few minutes adjusting the gas wall heater in the dressing room.

On the day of the show, rain was bucketing down. Prudence and Phyllida left their hotel, dressed in long raincoats, hoods, and boots. They treated themselves to a London taxi, arriving at 7 for the 7:30 performance. The red carpeted lobby with gold walls was already crowded. The audience was largely middle-age and up. The women presented their tickets and were directed to stairs for the top balcony. They climbed three flights of stairs.

Behind them, as they climbed to their seats, Felicia Friday followed with a last-minute ticket. On a hunch, she had waited outside the Palladium, watching for Prudence. She suspected Prudence would take this opportunity to see Amadeus. Her seat at the back of the balcony made watching Prudence difficult, so Felicia edged closer as she noticed vacant seats. After the intermission, she was able to watch the show and watch Prudence. She leaned forward to photograph Prudence as she was rapturously watching Amadeus.

Amadeus' nostalgic show recreated many of his hits that made him such a star. He was known at the Scottish Elvis. He was dapper in his tuxedo with plaid lapels and a red silk shirt. His singing voice was slightly deeper than his youthful tones, and his wild gyrations were replaced by choreographed dance steps, but still Prudence and Phyllida were transported to their happy days in Oxford. They tapped their feet to the music and hugged each other as he sang favorites from their Oxford days.

Phyllida sensed something odd to her right. As she turned her head, she saw Felicia Friday with her phone ready to take a picture. Without disturbing Prudence, she raised her coat and hood to block Felicia's view. *That obnoxious woman! Why does she want to torment Prudence?*

At the end of the show, thunderous applause continued for several minutes. Amadeus did an encore of "Love Me," his opening song. Suddenly, the lights came on and the audience moved to stairs at the back of the hall. These metal stairs were both a quick exit to the back alley and a fire escape exit, as well as a back door entrance to the Palladium.

Amadeus hosted his friends, fans, and family in his dressing room. As the crowd thinned, Amadeus switched from Champagne to single malt whiskey. Florence received a call and departed suddenly, leaving her husband with William, both drunk and asleep in giant chairs in the dressing room. The heater was on to counter the cold damp of the rainy evening.

The next morning, the cleaning crew at the Palladium gently knocked on the dressing room assigned to Amadeus. It was not unusual for the entertainers to sleep over in their dressing rooms. The head stagehand used a pass key to gently open the door. The two men were asleep in their chairs. Their faces were flushed cherry red.

"Blimey!" shouted the stagehand. "Turn off that bloody heater. Help! Call 999. Now, help me open the door! Let's carry these men to the alley. That damned heater may have done its worst!"

Sirens became louder as they approached. The Palladium employees attempted to resuscitate the men. William started to moan and began to move. Amadeus was dead.

Train to Scotland

The train for Scotland left London at 7:30 a.m. the morning after the Palladium concert. Phyllida made Prudence pinky swear to be fully packed the night before, so she reluctantly agreed to wear the same clothes in the morning. The women left the hotel via taxi at 6:30 a.m. for King's Cross Station. It was an 8-hour trip to Inverness plus an hour by bus to Portree, Skye. The women settled into first class seats and requested tea from the steward. They carried sandwiches from the hotel to eat on their journey. They were both tired and excited.

"It was a great show last night, Philly. I'm so glad you agreed to go with me. I wouldn't have attended by myself. Amadeus has aged well, don't you think?"

"Yes, the man looks good. The music took me back to Oxford thirty years ago."

As the train left London and gained speed, the motion lulled the women to sleep. When they awoke, they were in rural England, with rolls of hay stacked in the mowed fields.

Rolling into Glasgow station was a welcome stop, allowing them to get off the train and walk around. Prudence remembered a jewelry shop she wanted to visit. Phyllida wanted a long walk and a latte. As they stepped onto the platform, Prudence spotted the jewelers.

"Wonderful! There's my store."

"Do you want something if I find a Starbucks?"

"Yes, a latte. Have a good walk, Philly."

Luckily, Phyllida found a Starbucks inside the station near her train's platform and then wandered through a newsstand on her way back to the train. A headline made her stop in her tracks.

AMADEUS FOUND DEAD IN PALLADIUM DRESSING ROOM

Dear God! Prudence will faint when she sees this. Phyllida purchased the paper and tucked it into her large purse as she rushed to the train.

Prudence met her at the platform. "Look, Philly, I found these lovely silver hoops with Celtic knots. I also bought a lovely pair of large amethyst studs. What luck!"

"Great. Let's get back to our seats and settle before the rush of new passengers."

Phyllida gave Prudence her latte and allowed the train to move away from Glasgow before easing the newspaper out of her purse. "Pru, dear, there's some very bad news in this newspaper."

As Prudence looked at the headlines, she paled. A trickle of tears started down her cheeks. "Philly, this is awful. We saw Amadeus just last night. He was strong, talented, so full of life. The paper says there was a faulty heater in the dressing room. The Palladium couldn't be that careless, could they?"

"I am so sorry, Pru." Phyllida held her friend's hand as Prudence continued to cry softly. "We can alter the trip any way you want, or we can spend our planned time in Skye. Whatever feels right to you."

Meanwhile, in London at the *London Daily Times*, Felicia Friday hoped to take advantage of the early morning news of Amadeus' death. She went into the editor's office to tell him she had attended the previous night's performance. "Sir, I have been following the American woman who's the mother of Amadeus' love child. She's currently in London, and in fact, she attended last night's performance. Coincidentally, she exited the fire escape stairs that pass right by the entrance to the Palladium dressing rooms."

The young, newly hired editor needed a good story. "Great, write this up! Oh, I see you have photos, even better. Have this ready for the noon edition."

While the noon edition hadn't yet reached Glasgow, it had reached the London constabulary after Prudence Silver left on the train for Inverness. The train made no stops between Glasgow and Inverness; however, the head conductor was alerted that the two American women, Prudence Silver and Phyllida Walker, should be detained for questioning. As the train stopped in Inverness, a tall grey-haired man, Superintendent Marcus Jones, and mid-twenties woman with short brown hair and bright blue eyes, Sergeant Ann MacLeod, entered the first-class car and sat beside Prudence and Phyllida to announce that they would be accompanying them to Portree for questioning regarding the death of Amadeus.

Prudence, her eyes swollen, was too stunned to speak. Phyllida decided that silent compliance was best. Officer Jones lifted down their luggage and assisted the women off the train and into a grey, unmarked SUV for the drive to Portree, Skye.

The sun was fading in the late afternoon as Superintendent Jones began the drive. Phyllida and Prudence sat silently in the backseat.

The drive proceeded south with the sun setting in the west. A surreal rose gold glowed on low rolling hills as they traveled the well-paved highway that bordered the ocean.

"Have you ladies ever been to Skye?"

Both women shook their heads "no" as they remained in stunned silence.

"My family and I conduct tours of Skye. 'Tis a fascinating island with considerable history. Is this why you planned a visit here? The B&B you chose is the best in Portree, by the way. Wonderful food."

"A travel agent made our reservations." Phyllida spoke to relieve the stifling silence.

Prudence continued to dab at tears and sniff into a well-used tissue. Sergeant MacLeod handed her a box of tissues. Prudence managed a weak, "Thanks," as she took several.

The drive continued across a long bridge, then over a rocky landscape with low growing shrubs. They drove north along a narrow two-lane road by the water. Fog and drizzle were misting the air as they neared Portree.

"We're approaching Portree, ladies. The London constabulary

has questions about Amadeus' death, but I think they'll hold until tomorrow. You're free to settle into your rooms, unpack, and dine this evening. I'll pick you up after breakfast, about 10 a.m. tomorrow."

"Are we under arrest?" Phyllida spoke up.

"No, I've been asked to detain you for questioning about Amadeus' death under questionable circumstances. That news article made accusations that we will have to sort out."

"That ghastly reporter, Felicia Friday! Why is she stalking me?" Prudence was angry as color returned to her pale face.

"Trust me and my sergeant to uncover the truth." Sergeant MacLeod nodded in agreement. "Here we are at your B&B. I'll get someone to carry your bags and check you in. I'll return in the morning. There's a langoustine special this evening. You should try it."

The women provided the voucher for their adjoining rooms. The hotelier, a woman with bright red hair, wore a green plaid uniform. "Welcome to Portree Bed and Breakfast. I see you're booked for 10 days with breakfast and supper included. We hope you enjoy your stay on this lovely Scottish Island. Feel free to take an assortment of brochures for planning trips. I can arrange car rentals by the day if you wish."

Phyllida managed a courteous smile as she took the keys. "I hear there's a special dinner tonight. What time?"

"Yes, indeed. We have a langoustine special this evening, and you can go to the dining room between 17:30 and 21:00. Just choose a table and we'll take your order."

Prudence and Phyllida took the elevator to the third floor and discovered their luggage already in their rooms. They left the connecting door open so they could talk as they unpacked. Prudence placed a cold washcloth on her eyes to reduce the redness. Then they went to the dining room, which was papered in green plaid with antlers and mounted fish adorning the walls. Large windows revealed the North Atlantic pounding the cliffs nearby.

To accompany their seafood, the women ordered a carafe

of Riesling. The langoustine was delicious, with small potatoes, carrots, and leeks prepared perfectly.

"I didn't realize I was famished until I began eating." Prudence dabbed a napkin – serviette in the UK – to her lips. "I wonder if everyone here knows we're murder suspects, Philly."

"If they know, they're not giving us much attention, Pru. Considering this is Amadeus' hometown, we're going to get plenty of notice before the end of ten days."

"Maybe we should plan to leave as soon as Superintendent Jones finishes with us. The rooms are great, though. Your travel agent did a great job booking us in Portree. Be sure to let her know. We should take her to lunch when we get home."

Portree, Skye

The two women slept soundly their first night in Portree. They were both mentally and physically exhausted. Phyllida woke at 6 a.m. She knew breakfast started at 6:30, giving her time for a short walk to see Portree in daylight. Prudence was reading in bed and watching the morning show. Amadeus' untimely death was the main topic of news, with pictures of his wife and four children.

"No mention of that ghastly Felicia Friday article, thank God. Enjoy your walk, Philly. I'll meet you in the dining room around 7."

Outside, the cool mist of fog felt wonderful on Phyllida's face. Her silver hair swept up into a halo of curls. She saw one- and two-story buildings in a variety of pastel colors, and store windows with Celtic and Nordic books, maps, and figurines. Clothing shops displayed rain jackets, Wellingtons, and Isle of Sky logos. Seagulls were squawking near the harbor, hoping for fish from the early morning catch.

Returning to the B&B, Phyllida stepped to the dining room entrance to look for Prudence. "Over here, Philly," Prudence called and waved. She was sitting with a French press of coffee still brewing. The room was warm and inviting with the smell of coffee, tea, and fresh baked bread.

"What a charming little town!" Phyllida read the chalkboard menu across the room. "The aroma of the fresh baked rolls is so enticing. I'll have a brown raisin bun with hot tea."

"After breakfast, I think I'll take a walk around town to clear my head before Superintendent Jones comes to pick us up. On TV they say Amadeus' body will arrive today and be taken by hearse down the high street from the airport to the mortuary. What an awful way to die!" Prudence's eyes reddened and her voice shook as she spoke.

"His family and fans are grieving, and I'm devastated." Phyllida nodded as a young woman placed her tea pot and bun on the table. "Such a pleasant little inn in spite of our circumstances."

"Wonder what we should wear for our interrogation?"

"Casual, so we look like any other tourist."

After time to freshen up and dress, the two women returned to the lobby at 9:50. "Oh, ladies, Superintendent Jones is in the dining room."

Superintendent Jones was finishing a full Scottish breakfast – eggs, sausage, bacon, tomatoes, beans, potatoes, and fried bread with a strong pot of tea to wash it down. A young waitress approached his table. "Want more hot water for your tea, Dad?"

"Hello ladies, this is my daughter, Meghan. Want to join me for some tea or coffee?"

Meghan gave a polite smile as she prepared to take their orders.

"A cup of tea for me, dear. You have a lovely daughter, Superintendent Jones." Prudence smiled. "Nice to meet you, Meghan."

"I'll have a cup of tea as well, Meghan. Thanks so much. I had no idea your daughter worked here, Superintendent." Phyllida placed a serviette on her lap.

"This is the first I have seen you ladies smile. You're not under arrest." Superintendent Jones smiled as well.

When they'd all finished their tea, Marcus Jones drove the women to the police station, a grey stone two-story building with a commemorative plaque stating it was built in 1896.

As they entered the station, Sergeant Ann MacLeod directed Phyllida down the hall, and Superintendent Jones showed Prudence to a nearby interview room. He turned on the recording device on the table. A London paper stuck out of a thin file on the table.

"Just to clear the air, Mrs. Silver, you don't seem the type to murder."

"No, I'm not a murderer, Sir."

"Are you the mother of a child fathered by Amadeus?"

"Yes, my daughter, Vanessa, was fathered by Amadeus. This all happened when I was young, naïve, and stupidly in love. When Amadeus discovered I was pregnant, he gave me money for a termination. At the same time, I learned that he had eloped with his current wife, who was also expecting."

"You must have considerable resentment for the man's bad behavior."

"I was devastated and angry. I returned home to San Francisco with Phyllida's help. I married the boyfriend I had left behind – a wonderfully decent man. Vanessa's birth was declared premature. My husband was a wonderful father. He died never knowing the truth about Amadeus being Vanessa's father."

"What made you decide to seek out Amadeus at this time? I have a copy of a letter with pictures that you sent him two months ago."

Prudence straightened in her chair before answering. "My husband had died, so I didn't have to worry about hurting him. Vanessa is an accomplished ballerina with the San Francisco Ballet. She has her father's platinum hair and artistic talent. I felt it was time to tell her the truth. I wanted Amadeus to realize what an accomplished daughter he had. Vanessa's very angry with me, by the way."

"Do you have any idea who the person is making innuendos on Facebook?"

"I don't know for sure, but I suspect it's that awful reporter, Felicia Friday."

"Well, I can assure you that we checked and "Anonymous" is not Felicia Friday."

"I have no idea in that case."

"When you attended Amadeus' performance at the Palladium, did you plan on trying to see him?"

"Absolutely not! I sat in the balcony and made no attempt to do anything other than listen to him sing. I exited as everyone in that section of the balcony was directed. I have no idea where the stage door is or how to get into that part of the theater."

Phyllida was led to a second interview room where Sergeant MacLeod sat opposite her and turned on a tape recorder. "Mrs. Walker, how long have you known Mrs. Silver?"

"It must be over thirty years now. Prudence and I were roommates at nursing college in Oxford. We loved going to the pub where there was live entertainment. Frequently, Amadeus and his group sang there."

"Why did you move from England to San Francisco, if I may ask?"

"I traveled to San Francisco when Prudence returned home pregnant and devastated by Amadeus' abandonment. I became part of a wedding party in the marriage to Prudence's local boy-friend, George Silver. I met my future husband, Robert Walker, Prudence's cousin. I became an immigrant and new wife in one swoop. My only daughter, Beth, and Pru's daughter, Vanessa, are cousins and great friends."

"We noticed that you and Prudence both had pepper spray in your purses. Why is that?"

"In San Francisco, I foolishly walked across a public park after dark and three young thugs attacked me and snatched my purse. I was knocked to the ground, hit my head on a rock, and spent the night in the hospital with cuts and bruises. Pru and I decided to take a self-defense course, which included how to use pepper spray."

"I see – probably good idea to be cautious in the UK as well. Even Portree has the occasional purse snatch. Thank you for your patience as we gather information." Sergeant MacLeod quietly folded the file over her written notes, turned off the recorder, and stood up.

Phyllida met Prudence in the front office with Superintendent Jones.

"Ladies, I'm in a bit of a rush to get you back to your B&B. I'm part of the cortege that will honor Amadeus' return to Skye."

The ride to the B&B was silent. This was the first time the women had seen Portree open for business. The sidewalks were inhabited with tourists, exploring the many shops. The aroma of the sea, pubs, and tea shops blended in the cool air. Views of the churning ocean flashed between buildings.

"I can't sit still. Let's explore the shops along the main street." Phyllida buttoned up her sweater. Prudence simply followed along silently.

The shops intrigued the women as they searched for Skye mementos. As they moved from shop to shop, people began gathering along the sidewalks. Looking onto the street, they saw Superintendent Jones driving slowly in a police van with blue lights flashing, followed by a black hearse with flowers almost obscuring the casket. Cars and vans of local mourners followed to the Portree Chapel of Rest.

Prudence, unable to look away, quickly put on her sunglasses. Her mouth trembled and a few tears rolled down her cheeks. She offered a silent prayer for the man she once loved.

Phyllida stood next to Prudence as she thought about Amadeus' life, so unexpectedly lost in what she prayed was an unfortunate accident and not murder.

Down the street, a photographer captured these women solemnly watching Amadeus' passing cortege.

Felicia Friday in Skye

Felicia Friday urged her supervisor to send her to Skye to cover the funeral of Amadeus. She pointed out that the two suspicious women were already there.

"I might have an original scoop on the murder charges, Sir!"

"Worth a try I suppose. Someone should cover the funeral. Mind, don't make any wild accusation like you did with Camilla Mackenzie and Johnny MacKay! Tread softly, softly. I'm still receiving complaints from outraged Amadeus fans."

"Of course not, Sir." Felicia tucked her head modestly as she left the room.

Grand! Now I can continue my coverage of Amadeus. Pity he died, though. I had hoped to continue covering him through the years. Now, I'll just shadow those two women until one of them is arrested.

Expenses did not allow Felicia to stay at the same B&B as Prudence and Phyllida. She rented a room further inland and hired a car. Luckily, she was present to view the cortege moving down the high street and photograph Prudence and Phyllida pensively watching. This picture appeared in the next day's newspaper.

Final Return to Skye

Florence was in a state of shock when she learned her husband had died in the Palladium dressing room. A tearful and panicked phone call to her father brought the Reverend Malcolm MacDonald flying to London to assist his daughter. Thankfully, he helped her through the entanglements of returning Amadeus home to Skye and preparing for his funeral. He carefully steered Florence away from viewing the casket as it was loaded onto the private plane from London to Portree. For the solemn drive down Portree's High Street, the grief-stricken children, Llewellyn, Fergus, and Eric rode in the limousine beside their mother while the youngest, Malcolm, sat in the next limousine beside his grandfather. The hearse carrying Amadeus was so full of flowers that the casket was nearly buried from sight.

In the Chapel of Rest, Florence oversaw the arrangement of flowers around Amadeus in his red plaid tartans. He looked very handsome, as though asleep. Florence offered a prayer and felt Amadeus would approve of the opulent display.

The following day, the family attorney was scheduled to meet with Florence, her father, and her four children. Percy Olin Fraser III, known as Trey, was the third generation with the Portree Law Firm. Recently, he began handling all his father's cases, including Amadeus' current revisions to his will. He wore his three-piece grey suit to emphasize his professional position. Amadeus had revised his will recently in a way that might shock the wife and children. Trey hoped they would handle it without too much alarm.

When Trey arrived promptly at 2 p.m., Reverend MacDonald was waiting to open the door. "My condolences to you, your daughter, and grandchildren, Sir."

The Reverend had taught Trey's catechism and confirmation classes. He noted how professional this once mischievous, overactive boy now looked.

"Right through to the great room."

Trey smiled a greeting to all and placed his chair facing the family. "I've known all of you most of my life, and I feel a great sorrow at the passing of your talented husband and father." As he placed his open case on the floor and removed a file, he cleared his throat. "There is a delicate matter to attend to. I don't know if any of you are aware that Amadeus recently altered his will. Fergus MacCann, Amadeus, left a legacy to Ms. Vanessa Silver, his acknowledged daughter by Prudence Walker Silver. We will need to have Vanessa Silver present as well as her mother, Prudence Silver, before I can read the will. I can assure you that all of you present will be favorably compensated by Amadeus' estate."

Florence grasped the arms of her chair as her stomach churned. "Perhaps I should have been prepared for this, but I'm shocked."

"Again, my condolences to all of you. Amadeus was a great man and will be missed."

Llewellyn, sitting next to Florence, held her mother's hand.

Young Fergus stood up and shouted, "There needs to be proof. I want a DNA test!"

"Google her, Fergus, you'll see the resemblance, son." Florence spoke softly.

Eric and Malcolm looked at each other in confusion.

"What's going on, Mom?" Eric turned to face his mother.

"Your dad had an affair before he married me. I was waiting for the right time to tell you that he fathered a daughter by her."

Malcolm pulled out his phone and googled Vanessa Silver. "Wow, she looks like Llewellyn's twin, only thinner. Bloody hell!"

The Reverend MacDonald rose to the rescue and announced, "I think we should toast Amadeus, then enjoy this tea while digesting this news." He waved his hand over the table with a high tea of small sandwiches, cakes, and fruits as he spoke. "Trey, anything we need to tend to today?"

"I need Mrs. MacCann to sign a few documents so she can access part of the money to maintain her current lifestyle and manage any outstanding bills. Amadeus left a well-managed estate."

"Who's going to get in touch with this Vanessa Silver?" Fergus growled.

Trey stood as he said, "I've made arrangements to notify Ms. Silver and her mother." At this point, Trey saluted Amadeus with a glass of sherry. He moved to each family member, giving an individual condolence and handshake before leaving.

From his car, Trey called Superintendent Jones to arrange a meeting with Prudence Silver and her travel mate, Phyllida Walker. He would treat all of them to dinner at a posh restaurant.

The MacCann family listened for Trey to drive away; then all began talking.

"I want DNA proof. People can resemble without being related." Fergus' voice rose above the rest.

Florence took a deep breath, then began speaking softly, "There is DNA proof. Vanessa Silver has two young sons, and one had a condition common to Nordic people. It can be confused with leukemia. Luckily for the child, there is enough Viking in the Mac-Cann family to reassure the child's condition only required an iron supplement. You had the same condition, Malcolm. Remember we had special drops we put in your orange juice?"

"I do indeed! I still don't like orange juice."

Llewellyn spoke pensively as she looked at the latest MacCann family portrait with the four children gathered around Amadeus and Florence. "Vanessa contacted Dad because she had a sick baby boy. I can understand that; I would do the same. Gosh! Vanessa is a talented dancer and mother of two. Evidently, she inherited our father's talent and high energy."

"I'm going to rest for a while. Cook will prepare dinner for 19:00." Florence rose from her chair and looked as tired as she sounded.

Dinner at the Portree Arms

Superintendent Jones phoned Prudence and invited the two travelers to dinner. He didn't mention that the dinner was hosted by Solicitor Trey Fraser, who was managing Amadeus' estate.

Maybe a couple of sherries before requesting a command appearance by Vanessa Silver, mused Superintendent Jones.

"My wife, Helen, will be accompanying me. She loves the Portree Arms. They're famous for wonderful food. Prince Charles has eaten there. Shall we pick you up about 19:00?"

"You know, Philly, this dinner invitation sounds too good to be true. Hope no strings are attached."

"Well, I'm looking forward to a fine dinner. You think my outfit for our London tea will do?"

"It'll have to do for me as well. Those are the only dress clothes I brought since someone insisted I pack light." Prudence raised an eyebrow toward Phyllida.

"Touché. But we have sufficient clothing. Maybe the dinner is a sort of apology for our being accused of Amadeus' death."

"That's a possibility. Let's have a light supper and an early evening tonight. All these big meals will keep me from fitting into my new black jeans."

Superintendent Jones telephoned Trey Fraser. "Afternoon, Trey, Mrs. Silver and Mrs. Walker are willing to meet you for dinner at the Portree Arms tomorrow night at 19:30. Shall I make the reservations? Is your girlfriend coming?"

Trey knew he had been taken advantage of by Superintendent Jones. He intended to write it off as a necessary business expense. "Certainly, I'll bring Fiona. The ladies will enjoy all the jovial company."

I'm not worried about having the ladies meet Fiona. They are San Franciscans.

The women looked elegant as they waited for Superintendent Jones. They didn't notice Felicia Friday hiding in a chair behind a newspaper. She had been attempting to track Prudence for two days now. She strained to eavesdrop.

"I looked up the Portree Arms today. Their menu looks elegant and expensive." Phyllida showed Prudence the menu on her phone. "I'm looking forward to the Oysters Flambe."

"I'll have trouble deciding. Everything looks wonderful. Here's Superintendent Jones."

"May I present my wife, Helen Jones. Dear, this is Phyllida Walker and Prudence Silver."

"I've heard so much about you ladies. I feel I already know you." Helen was wearing a long Paisley skirt and black turtleneck with a silver pendant necklace. Her wavy auburn hair was shoulder length.

Jones led the three women to his personal car, a blue Lexus sedan.

Felicia Friday looked up the Portree Arms for its address and menu. *Damn, this is going to be expensive. Maybe I can just sit at the bar and watch.*

Trey Fraser and Fiona were just walking to the entrance when Superintendent Jones and the three women pulled up. They walked into the restaurant together. Fiona Clark stood slightly taller than Trey with her stiletto heels. Her platinum hair was straight to her shoulders with long bangs. A black and silver pantsuit showed off a very slender figure.

They sat three across with each man between two women. Trey managed to sit next to Prudence and took the lead in ordering for the table.

"Shall we start with a Prosecco and steamed clams? It's a specialty here."

"Sounds wonderful to me," Prudence and Phyllida spoke together.

Everyone laughed, including the waiter.

Fiona sat directly across from Prudence and leaned forward as she spoke, "Darling, your haircut is just wonderful. It reminds me of the 1920s. Those pearl earrings dangle just below your hair."

Fiona reached her perfectly manicured hand to touch one of the pearl earrings.

Prudence used willpower not to shiver from the bold hand at her ear. She recognized the deep voice as a man who had transitioned to a woman. With a sweet smile, Prudence put her hand to her earring as she spoke. "Thank you, Fiona. These earrings are a cherished gift."

Superintendent Jones quickly spoke up, "Fiona is Skye's local veterinarian."

"I'm the only vet on the island. Cousin Amadeus paid for my schooling and was supportive until I came out as a woman. You notice I have the trademark platinum hair. I cut and styled it myself. I understand your daughter, Vanessa Silver, has our trademark hair as well. I can hardly wait to meet her." Fiona suddenly jumped from Trey's sharp kick to her shin.

"Are you planning on traveling to San Francisco?" Prudence asked with a puzzled look.

"We are great fans of ballet, all dance, actually. We travel frequently for performances." Trey spoke while raising an eyebrow at Fiona. "We've just started attending the local Scottish Country Dance."

"We do indeed," mumbled Fiona, giving attention to buttering a roll.

Felicia Friday managed to find a seat at the bar where she could see Prudence, but she could hear nothing. She ordered oysters, which she hoped to eat slowly enough to catch some phrases from the dinner party. Something interesting was going on between Prudence and the woman with the long blond hair. *Was this Amadeus' daughter? Let me look up a photo of the family on my phone. No, not Llewellyn. Hmm.*

Phyllida sat across from Helen. "Mrs. Walker, you have the most beautiful curly hair. Is it natural?"

"Yes, and please call me Phyllida. Are you a native of Skye?"

"Yes, I am. My family, the MacQueen clan, is one of the oldest families on Skye. In fact, Amadeus won his estate from a distant MacQueen relative in a card game."

"What?"

"Quite true," volunteered Fiona.

The meal continued with everyone enjoying a medley of seafood caught that day with fresh, crisp broccoli rabe and potatoes mashed with parsnips. Just before dessert, Trey raised his voice as he held up a wine glass. "I have some very good news, Mrs. Silver. Amadeus remembered you and your daughter in his will. There will be a reading of the will on the afternoon after the funeral. You and your daughter, Vanessa, are required to be present before the will can be read. I sent a certified letter to Vanessa with assurance that all her travel expenses for herself and her husband will be covered. Your expenses will be covered as well," he hastily added.

Prudence felt herself grow faint as the words sank in. "You contacted Vanessa? What was her answer?"

"I had a colleague from Stanford hand deliver the letter. Your daughter was obviously caught by surprise and promised to get back to me by tomorrow."

"Good heavens!" was all Prudence could manage to say.

"Anyone want dessert? They have frozen fruit gelatos – lemon and cantaloupe sorbet in the shape of that fruit, spectacular!" Trey spoke heartily even as he saw Prudence and Phyllida looking shocked and unhappy. "The Fraser family plan is to be more welcoming than you might expect. Particularly the eldest daughter, Llewellyn."

"You might want to stay clear of Fergus, Jr. He's been grumbling." Fiona received another kick to the shins. "Well, he has said some nasty things, and these two lovelies need to be more prepared than surprised."

Somehow, Trey unobtrusively paid the bill. Everyone retrieved their coats and moved to their cars quietly. Prudence grumbled into Phyllida's ear, "Remind me to turn down the next offer of a fancy dinner."

"Darling," Phyllida took her friend's arm as she whispered, "I've got your back."

Vanessa's Secret

"Dear God, Yuri, how do I explain this to your mother?" Vanessa waved the hand delivered letter as she spoke. "How will this affect my career? I cringe at this kind of publicity."

"Well, Lubchik, I have a surprise for you. My mother was an avid Amadeus fan. She even joined his fan club. Her reaction might amaze you."

"Really? First, I find out that my father is not George Silver. Then I'm asked to travel overseas. I'm the bastard at this family gathering. Will you come with me to Skye? You may need to prevent me from killing my crazy, beautiful mother."

"Of course. But first we need to see if my parents will take care of the children."

"I hadn't even thought of that. Your mother was in an Amadeus fan club?"

"My mother flirted with my father because he looked like Amadeus! I've heard the story many times. I'll call to let my folks know we're coming over with the boys."

The Chermovsky family had immigrated to San Francisco when Yuri was ten. In an effort to assimilate, they studied English and read and spoke only English for four years, but when Yuri's grandparents finally emigrated from Odessa, the household became Russian again. Yuri was bilingual and interpreted for his grandparents. Purchasing a house in the Richmond District was a great accomplishment. They loved the Russian shops and other ethnic shops near their house, two blocks from Clement Street. Schubert's Bakery sold fresh Russian piroshki. A Russian pharmacy allowed the grandparents to speak about their health in their mother tongue. A large Chinese market provided the freshest vegetables straight from local farms. Cinderella Bakery offered a wonderful variety of Russian soups and baked goods, and the 2 Clement bus traveled downtown with a stop that was walking distance from home.

Yuri parked in the driveway and led his family through the kitchen door. A large pot of borscht was simmering on the stove. The house was warm and inviting with the aroma of soup, chicken stock, and freshly made pelmeni.

"Podroogie, so glad to see you. I've been cooking today. Please, come sit and join us for an early supper." Bella Chermovsky was a short, energetic woman, recently retired from her work at the Jewish Community Center where she'd helped Russian Jewish emigres adapt to life in America.

Yuri and Vanessa dutifully sat down to bowls of red borscht with a dollop of sour cream and dill on top. Ivan and Dimitry sat in booster chairs, eating borscht in swan bowls, assisted by Granddad Mikhail. After they had eaten and the dishes were cleared, Yuri cleared his throat before speaking. "You remember Amadeus, the Scottish singer, don't you?"

"Of course, that's why I flirted with Misha," Bella smiled and patted her husband's arm.

"When Vanessa's mother, Prudence, was studying in England, Amadeus was singing at a local pub. They became acquainted, more than acquainted. Amadeus is Vanessa's father."

Bella and Mikhail sat stunned for a minute. "Bozhe moi," Bella exclaimed. "My God!"

"Why are we just learning this?" Mikhail asked, taking Bella's hand.

"Vanessa just learned it too. Prudence led George to believe he was Vanessa's father."

"It seems that Amadeus, who recently died, left Vanessa and Prudence an inheritance." Yuri took a breath before continuing. "Vanessa and Prudence are required to be present at the reading of the will in Scotland. Portree on the Isle of Skye to be exact – in about ten days. Amadeus' estate will cover all the travel expenses for both of us. Is it possible for you to care for the boys while we are gone?"

"Of course, we'll care for the boys!" Bella and Mikhail exclaimed together. "Where is Prudence, by the way?"

"She's already in Portree, traveling with her friend, Phyllida. You heard about Amadeus' death possibly being murder? It seems Prudence and Phyllida must remain until the investigation is complete." Yuri prayed they wouldn't ask if Prudence and Phyllida were murder suspects. Thankfully, they didn't.

Vanessa nervously clasped and unclasped her fingers in the silence.

"You mean Ivan and Dimitry, my grandchildren, are Amadeus' grandchildren too?"

"Our grandchildren, Bella," Mikhail clarified. Everyone watched the two boys playing on the rug by the table. The family tidied the kitchen together and then watched the news.

"Can you make a list of the children's schedule and medications? Are they okay to sleep in twin beds?" Bella asked. "Also, Mikhail and I must be listed as authorized to pick up Ivan at the preschool."

"You're already authorized, Mother Bella," Vanessa assured her. "I have a bed rail for Dimitry that Yuri and I will bring over with their clothes and some favorite toys."

"How about bringing them over two days early? We can make sure we have everything we need, and you might find it easier to pack." Bella spoke while helping Dimitry into his jacket. She ruffled his hair and kissed his cheek as she led him to Yuri.

Granddad Mikhail helped Yuri put the boys in their car seats. He affectionately put a hand on Yuri's shoulder. Bella and Mikhail waved from the driveway as the family drove away.

"Yuri, you were wonderful with your parents. I'm so relieved to have all of this out in the open. George Silver will always be my father, but I am curious about my Scottish heritage." Vanessa took Yuri's arm as they walked to their bedroom after putting the boys to bed.

"Of course, you're curious, Lubchik. At some point you'll need to make peace with your mother. She gave you a wonderful childhood, you know."

"Yes, she did, but I still resent all the secrecy. My dad, George, probably would have married her anyway."

"You can't be sure of that. Try not to get tied in knots about what could or should have been." Yuri hugged his wife as they readied themselves for an early night.

The next ten days passed in a blur. Yuri and Vanessa had traveled frequently with the San Francisco Ballet company and packing was easy, but Vanessa was full of nerves. "Do I attend the funeral, and should I wear black?"

"You know how to dress, Lubchik."

"I'm not trying to stand out, Yuri. I just want to be present and kind for what will probably be the only meeting with my father's family. I wonder how Mother is going to feel during the funeral and will reading?"

"She's probably just as nervous as you are."

The Late-Night Flight to Portree

Yuri and Vanessa flew business class from San Francisco to Glasgow on British Air. They had comfortable seats that reclined for sleeping. They felt rested when the plane lights turned on to simulate morning and breakfast was served.

Vanessa stepped into the aisle, holding the seat back and began to stretch. After a few gentle stretches backward and forward, she raised each leg directly over her head. Then she bent forward at the waist to touch her palms to the carpet. Passengers in nearby seats watched in amazement.

"I hear that this woman is a famous ballerina."

"She must be. No ordinary human could do that!"

Unaware of the amazement she'd created, Vanessa settled into her seat to eat her vegetable omelet. "I could get used to this."

"Wonder how we make our way to the private plane to Portree?" Yuri finished his bagel with smoked salmon.

Just after the plane landed, announcements began. "Welcome to Glasgow International Airport. European citizens should follow the blue line to British Border Control. All other passengers should follow the green line. Mr. and Mrs. Chermovsky, an ambassador will meet you when you exit British Border Control."

A uniformed woman with a Glasgow International Ambassador name tag held a sign for Mr. and Mrs. Chermovsky. Yuri and Vanessa introduced themselves, and she led them to a motorized transporter. "Welcome to Scotland. I'll escort you to your plane for Portree."

She took them on a ten-minute ride through the airport and out onto the tarmac where a private plane waited with its steps lowered. A man in a grey suit stood at the foot of the steps. He recognized the two dancers immediately. "Welcome to Scotland. I hope your flight was uneventful. I'm Percy Fraser, but please call me Trey. I'm the administrator of Amadeus' estate. We have a two-hour flight to Portree. As we're flying, I'll fill you in about Amadeus' family funeral arrangements and an informal meeting to be held with you. The children and widow plan to give you a cordial welcome and provide some of the Fergus MacCann family history. I must say, you have a striking resemblance to your half-sister, Llewellyn."

"I look forward to seeing my wife's twin." Yuri smiled. "Lubchik, I thought your beauty was exclusive."

Superintendent Jones was waiting at the small airstrip to pick up Trey and his clients. Yuri and Vanessa paused at the open door and looked at the wild rocky ground and breathed the cool, ocean air. Jones watched the two tall, blonde dancers resembling Nordic gods, taking in their first sight of the wild, rocky Isle of Skye. *Vanessa Silver certainly resembles her half-sister, Llewellyn. I wonder how they'll relate to each other.*

Superintendent Jones would deliver Vanessa and Yuri to the B&B where Prudence and Phyllida were waiting. Trey planned to act as host in introducing Amadeus' family on Skye later in the day, but first, he would let Vanessa and Prudence have some private time.

Prudence was nervously pacing in the lobby while Phyllida sat nearby in a plaid chair. A fragrant wood fire burned in the fireplace. The women didn't see Felicia Friday lurking behind a magazine rack. Trey led Vanessa and Yuri into the lobby and paused as Vanessa and Prudence rushed to hug.

"Darlings." Prudence released one arm to include Yuri in a group hug. "I am so sorry to involve you in this mess."

"I know, Mother." Vanessa, still hugging her mother, reached a hand to Phyllida, who was standing nearby. "My mother is so lucky to have a good friend like you, Aunty Philly."

Yuri smiled his agreement.

After a few minutes, Trey cleared his throat to get their attention. "We have a meeting with the Frasers at 16:30 with a buffet and drinks so you can become acquainted. You're invited to come as well, Mrs. Walker. The eldest, Llewellyn, has prepared a family album and genealogical history for Vanessa."

Phyllida turned to Prudence. "I'm going to take a little walk around town. I'll be back in time to meet the Frasers."

"Okay, friend, but promise me you'll stay close. Who could have imagined, so many years ago, when I was Amadeus' starstruck lover, what long range consequences our relationship would have?"

Behind the Scenes

Phyllida loved traveling with Prudence, but sometimes she needed some alone time. She had discovered a wooden bench behind shops that looked out on the harbor. The sound of the sea and the chatter of sea gulls created a meditative mood. In the distance, a tall, slender woman was walking a greyhound. *People do seem to resemble their pets. I think that's Fiona, Trey's friend. She really stands out in her neon pink jacket, sneakers, and pink rhinestone cap with that blond ponytail trailing from the cap. Oh my! The dog's wearing a pink rhinestone collar to match.*

Fiona waved and started coming towards her. "Phyllida! Hello! What a surprise to see you! May we join you?"

"Of course." Phyllida moved to make room.

The greyhound immediately pushed his muzzle into Phyllida's hand. "Hope you like dogs. This is Mercury, Merk for short. I rescued him after his racing days were over. He's a real love."

"I do like dogs." Phyllida unconsciously petted Merk's narrow head.

"I've been hoping to see you in private. A newspaper woman, Felicia Friday, has been trying to get an interview with me about our dinner a few days ago. She insinuated that you two are still suspects in Amadeus' death. Of course, I told her nothing. People working at your B&B have seen her hanging about, spying on you and Prudence."

"Oh God! I'm glad you told me. That woman's news article is the reason we were considered suspects. Pru and I will be very careful to stay away from her."

"Please don't tell Trey I told you about Ms. Friday. He thinks I talk too much."

"Well, I'm very grateful for the information, Fiona." Phyllida and Fiona stood at the same time. "Thanks for the tip. I won't tell Trey about our conversation."

"Glad to be helpful. Got to go. Merk is anxious for his dinner. Maybe we can get together for an afternoon tea sometime."

"I'd love that."

Fiona jogged downhill toward the harbor.

Phyllida walked briskly back to the B&B to warn Prudence that Felicia Friday was in Portree and stirring up trouble.

The Family Gathering

Trey arrived at the B&B 15 minutes early. He casually walked around the lounge area until he was beside a potted plant and facing Felicia Friday. "Ms. Friday, I'm Trey Fraser, attorney for Amadeus' estate. I represent all parties involved, including Prudence Silver, Phyllida Walker, and Vanessa Silver Chermovsky. I understand that you have been spreading rumors that Ms. Walker and Ms. Silver are still suspects in Amadeus' death. I'll be happy to sue both you and your employer for liable. Now, leave this B&B right now. Have I made myself clear?" Trey's voice had escalated to courtroom volume. "Off you go, now."

Felicia Friday looked wide eyed in surprise. "I can be wherever I want. This is a free country!"

"See the man in the blue Lexus at the passenger pick-up area? That's Superintendent Jones of the local constabulary. He will be following you and your rumor-mongering behavior very carefully. I'm warning you – stay away from these women! Now, get out!"

"I'm going." Felicia Friday angrily stomped away.

Superintendent Jones caught her eye and raised his eyebrows in a knowing way. *I'm going to keep an eye on you, Ms. Friday.*

Trey turned in time to greet Phyllida and Prudence exiting the elevator. "Afternoon, ladies. I just shooed off Felicia Friday."

"Who's that?" Vanessa and Yuri came from the stairwell in time to hear Trey's remark.

"We'll fill you in later. Too long to tell now," Prudence replied nervously.

"We'll be going in two cars. You can ride with Superintendent Jones." Trey led Vanessa and Yuri to the blue Lexus.

"Fiona is my chauffeur today." Trey pointed to the black Range Rover with Fiona at the wheel.

As Prudence and Phyllida entered the back seat, Fiona turned around to face them. "Hi, girls. I had second thoughts and told

Trey about Ms. Friday's spying. I would never forgive myself if you suffered from my silence."

Trey turned to face the back seat as he said, "I think I put a flea in Felicia Friday's bonnet about hanging around the B&B, but I want you to call me if you see her following you around town. Superintendent Jones is on guard as well. On to more pleasant matters, the MacCann family reserved the country club banquet room for this meeting. Amadeus was a founding member, and they're all very eager to meet you. There are no hard feelings. Nobody thinks you two women had anything to do with Amadeus' death."

Superintendent Jones greeted Vanessa and Yuri and invited them to sit in the back seat. "We're going to Amadeus' club. By the way, my family often act as tour guides. While you're in Portree, they'd be happy to show you around. My twin brother, Mattias, belongs to a group of Scottish Country Dancers, and he'd love to have you join them."

"I saw videos of Scottish dancing while preparing for a scene in Macbeth. A Scottish dance master came to a rehearsal to teach us authentic styling. We'd both love to join your brother." Yuri took Vanessa's hand as she smiled for the first time since arriving in Portree.

"The dancers meet every Tuesday evening at 19:30 at the Hare and Hound Inn. Mattias said he'd love to have you pros join his group."

"I look forward to meeting this group." Yuri put the date in his phone.

The Superintendent's car arrived first. He led Yuri and Vanessa to the banquet room, which was lined with hunting trophies of heavily antlered deer. Yuri was regal in black slacks, sweater, and a tweed jacket. Vanessa removed her black trench coat to reveal a black silk jumpsuit with a blue scarf decorated with angels. First in line was Llewellyn, who saw a reflection of herself in Vanessa's platinum hair and deep blue eyes. As the American guests moved down the line, they met Fergus, Eric, and finally, sixteen-year-old Malcolm. The Reverend Malcolm MacDonald stood beside

Florence, providing comfort for his daughter, Amadeus' widow.

The room hushed while all unobtrusively watched Florence and Prudence meet. As Prudence approached, the Reverend MacDonald reached his hand to shake hers and casually guided her to Florence.

Florence had heard that Prudence was beautiful. She saw the white-haired woman with slanted, turquoise eyes approaching. "You're just as pretty as rumors said."

"I'm so sorry for your loss, Florence. I truly wish you well. I've been a widow for over a year myself, and my friend, Phyllida, lost her husband two years ago."

"Yes, I did." Phyllida stepped up to take her hand. "My daughter was a great help in comforting me."

"My daughter and sons have been wonderful, and my father has assisted me with all the major decisions." Florence waved her hand towards the banquet display. "Please enjoy some refreshment. Amadeus always loved a party."

Trey led Phyllida and Prudence to a table and brought two glasses of chilled Riesling. He reappeared with a platter of chilled prawns and shelled langoustine with a vegetable medley.

Llewellyn invited Vanessa and Yuri to join her table to look through the album she'd created showing the history of the Mac-Cann family on the Isle of Skye.

Prudence's History of Felicia Friday

A few hours later when they returned to the B&B, Trey scouted the lounge for Felicia Friday. Happily, she was absent. Prudence and Phyllida suggested that Vanessa and Yuri come to Prudence's room for a chat. Phyllida had changed into her signature purple paisley lounge pants, sitting yoga-style on her bed. They all sipped chamomile tea as Prudence began sharing the Felicia Friday saga.

"When we arrived in London, we watched on telly as Felicia Friday was presenting a program about Amadeus, who was promoting his concert tour of England and Scotland. Felicia Friday, an awful woman, was sensationalizing Amadeus' womanizing history. The following day, as we searched for discount show tickets at Leicester Square, we realized Amadeus was appearing at the Palladium. We both wanted to hear him sing, for old times' sake, and chose balcony tickets. At the performance, Felicia Friday, who was apparently stalking us, took a photo of me during the performance. A few days earlier, she was at the Regency where we met Phyllida's cousins for high tea. While we were eating, she fainted from a diabetic episode, and Philly and I had to provide first aid.

"The morning after Amadeus' performance at the Palladium, we were on an early train to Scotland. During a stop, Philly picked up a newspaper with a front-page article, reporting Amadeus' death, written by Felicia Friday. I was heartsick to hear about the death of a man I had once loved. The article suggested that since I was at the Palladium show, I might be responsible for rigging the heater to cause the carbon monoxide death. Absolutely ridiculous! But as the train reached Inverness, Police Detective Superintendent Jones met Philly and me to escort us to our B&B in Portree. The next morning, we were taken to the Portree Police Station and formally interviewed."

"Oh my God!" Vanessa gasped.

"We had no idea you two were in such danger!" Yuri put his arm around Vanessa's shoulder.

"Superintendent Jones has emphasized that he considers Pru and me innocent, but we are under orders to remain in Portree until the mystery is solved."

"I'm staying here with you!" Vanessa hugged her mother as she spoke.

"I'm sure my parents will offer to keep the boys a little longer. I'll stay here too."

Everyone sat in pensive silence to watch the evening news on the telly before retiring to their rooms.

That same evening, Felicia Friday had a pub dinner at the Hare and Hound. She was in a quandary about preparing a news article on Amadeus' funeral without including some juicy items about Prudence. *Damn that Trey Fraser! Damn Fiona Clark, the perverted, big mouthed man/woman!*

Felicia had already promised her boss photos and news coverage at Amadeus' funeral this coming Saturday. Hopefully, she could photograph the famous bastard daughter and her handsome dancer husband attending the funeral. If she didn't get some enticing news soon, she would be in deep trouble.

At a table nearby, two couples were chatting as they drank their pints after the pub special of steak and ale pie.

"Mattias says that Vanessa Silver and Yuri Chermovsky will join our Scottish Country Dancing group this coming Tuesday. They're both soloists at the San Francisco Ballet. Should be fun to have these pros join us." The man spoke while sipping his ale.

"Oh, what fun! I'll bring my video to record their dancing," enthused his wife.

And I'll be there to video as well! Felicia ordered a half pint just so she could continue eavesdropping.

Amadeus' Funeral

The Reverend Malcolm MacDonald, a Church of England priest, had officiated at many funerals, but he was saddened by the death of his son-in-law, Amadeus. Furthermore, the extreme mourning of his daughter, Florence, and the four grandchildren hung heavy on his heart. The adoring fans with masses of flowers and social media condolences provided distraction, comfort, and, at times, comic relief.

The Reverend MacDonald began each morning with the morning prayer service in the 1662 Book of Common Prayer, either in his bedroom or, if weather permitted, in a beautiful garden. While staying with his daughter, he always sat on a wood bench at the edge of a field of wildflowers with the sea pounding the cliffs below. The sound of the sea provided a wonderful rhythm for his contemplation and prayers. In the last few days, a white-tailed sea eagle had been gliding over the cliffs with strength and agility that seemed to proclaim that life continues even during the sadness of an unexpected death.

St. Giles Church could accommodate 200 guests. The funeral attendance was by invitation only, and a large video screen in the church hall was provided for an overflow of mourners, plus selected members of the press, also by invitation only.

To her consternation, Felicia Friday couldn't get an invitation, but she managed to swipe an invitation from a local reporter, Hadley Whitcomb. Mr. Whitcomb left his press pass and invitation sticking out of his jacket pocket on a chair's back when he was at lunch. It was a jovial meet-up with many reporters arriving to cover Amadeus' funeral. Felicia stopped by to chat with colleagues after she liberated the pass poking out of Mr. Whitcomb's pocket.

Amadeus' family planned to visit the funeral home for a last viewing on Friday evening before the Saturday service. Church of England funerals were never open casket. This was the last opportunity to see Amadeus. Llewellyn called Vanessa and offered to drive her. Vanessa couldn't think of a kind or polite way to decline, even though the thought of seeing her father dead in a casket was repellant. Luckily, Yuri would be with her to lead her as she averted her gaze.

The mortuary had closed to visitors at noon to avoid disturbance by unruly fans. Florence arrived at the Portree Chapel of Rest first for some alone time with Amadeus. *Well, old boy, you should be pleased with the massive mounds of flowers. I chose the reddest MacDonald tartan for you. You look very handsome. Prudence is here with your daughter, Vanessa. Even with all your faults, I'm already missing you terribly. I would give so much just to hear you snore again.* Florence left before the children came in.

As Vanessa entered the chapel behind Llewellyn, she was bathed with the heavy scent of flowers. A large picture of Amadeus as a young star was the first thing she saw. *This must be how he looked when he and my mother were together.* Chills passed through her body. For the first time, she felt tears forming. She called on all her professionalism as a performer not to cry, but tears slid down her cheeks. She saw her father, an older man in red tartan, lying in his casket as if sleeping. She clung tightly to Yuri's arm as she walked away. In a distant corner, she observed Amadeus' children each stepping up to the casket. Some spoke to their father. Others just looked, and some made the sign of the cross.

As the family left the mortuary, Felicia Friday in a hooded black raincoat was standing at a distance. With a telephoto lens, she managed to photograph a somber looking Vanessa standing beside Llewellyn.

Trey visited the B&B later that day to deliver the funeral invitations. Phyllida and Prudence were relaxing near the fireplace.

"Phyllida, you're an honorary family member. I think it's important that you're present at the funeral and the reading of the will. Vanessa has Yuri beside her for support, and I think you'll provide a calming influence. Prudence is lucky to have your long-term friendship."

"Thank you, I was wondering how this would work out. I really feel for Pru, who grieves silently." Phyllida and Prudence gave each other a solemn look.

"This is such a strange situation, Philly. What an unexpected turn our trip has taken."

"So true, my friend. So true."

The women walked to the elevator as Vanessa and Yuri came into the lounge to meet Trey. He gave them their invitations and itinerary for Amadeus' funeral and will reading.

"Why do I have to attend the will reading, Trey?"

"Vanessa, you and your mother are mentioned in the will. I believe Amadeus attempted to acknowledge you and make amends."

"Oh, I didn't intend to ask for anything."

"No, but Amadeus intended to acknowledge you – even if belatedly. I'll be escorting you to the funeral tomorrow, along with Prudence and Phyllida. Fiona will be driving. She's relieved she didn't get an invitation for her distant cousin's funeral, by the way. Until tomorrow, then."

The Reverend MacDonald had thought about how to arrange the procession of immediate family following the casket into the church. He and Florence agreed that she would enter first beside her youngest son, Malcolm. Behind would be Amadeus' other children in order of age, with spouses. To Vanessa's great relief, Llewellyn was a month older. Vanessa and Yuri were third in line followed by Fergus, Jr., then Eric. Vanessa floated down the aisle, holding Yuri's arm, with a sad, stoic expression. She wore a black suit with pearls and her hair in a French braid, with a black silk ribbon at the nape of her neck.

The Reverend MacDonald led the casket as he intoned in a loud somber voice: "I am the resurrection and the life, saith the Lord: he that believeth in me, though he were dead, yet shall he live and whosoever liveth and believeth in me shall never die..."

Many musician friends of Amadeus were seated in the choir. The musicians cantered the service, providing the psalms and scripture in chant. Due to the length of this musical service,

Reverend MacDonald decided that there would be no sermon.

Trey, Prudence, and Phyllida sat in the row behind Amadeus' children. The women held tissues to stem the flow of tears during the solemn, beautiful service.

As mourners and press entered the church hall, Superintendent Jones was checking the passes and invitations. Felicia Friday, wearing a heavily veiled black hat, attempted to walk in a crowd, carrying her purloined pass, partially covered by her suit jacket.

Superintendent Jones spotted her and called to a nearby man, "Hadley, here's your missing pass. Ms. Friday, I should charge you, but I'll settle for your leaving the premises."

"As a member of the press, I have a right to cover this service. The public has a right to be informed. This is what I do for a living."

"The public will be properly informed, thank you. I have problems with your methods of getting news. Now, please leave."

Fiona was sitting in the car parked under a tree. With her phone, she videoed the episode for Trey. *He's going to love this.*

Felicia had prepared for such a problem. She walked around the block to her rental car and changed from the veiled black hat to a grey wig and a patterned black scarf that partially obscured her face. She waited behind a shrub and slipped in with a late arriving family, scurrying to enter before the service began. Fiona captured all of it on her phone.

The service ended with an inspirational duet of "You'll Never Walk Alone" by Johnny MacKay and Camilla Mackenzie. The solemn cadence of bagpipe and drum of the Portree Pipe and Drum Corps led family and mourners to the far end of the church cemetery where Amadeus was lowered to his grave alongside many departed MacCann relatives. The headstone left blank dates below Florence MacCann's name.

As the crowd milled around, greeting old acquaintances and relatives, Vanessa was approached by a buxom woman with unnaturally vivid red hair. "Actually, I was hoping to speak with you. I performed with your father before he became Amadeus. I'm a great fan of dance, ballet especially. I know Amadeus must have been proud of you."

Vanessa was unsure how to respond, but simply said, "Thank you."

Johnny MacKay managed to remain unseen as he took a picture of the two women in conversation. Later, as Camilla joined Johnny, he handed her the camera. "Here you go, Camilla. Hope you don't torture yourself with this."

"Thanks, Johnny. You've always had my back."

You have no idea, old girl, Johnny muttered to himself as they walked away.

These series of events were observed by plain clothes Portree police, who were videoing the funeral and burial. They would study the day's video of events very carefully back at headquarters.

Gratefully, the reading of the will was two hours after the conclusion of the funeral. This provided time for rest and reflection. Phyllida, Prudence, Vanessa, and Yuri returned to the B&B, and Trey and Fiona joined them for lunch. Fiona used this time to show the phone videos of Felicia's comical efforts to view the funeral.

"You can count on Felicia to publish some very damning innuendos about your continued presence in Portree and attendance at the funeral. She's a vile, nasty bitch. She's trying to justify her insinuations that made Prudence and Phyllida potential suspects in Amadeus' homicide in the first place."

"What does this horrible woman have against us?!" Prudence cried out, fighting tears as she almost tipped over her glass of water. She had declined wine to keep her head clear on this stressful day.

"Oh, it's not personal. She simply wants her share of fame and accolades," Fiona offered as she took a long drink of her wine. Fiona was the only person at the table drinking alcohol.

Amadeus' Last Will and Testament

Fiona drove everyone to Amadeus' home. The family had prepared for the reading of the will in the large room that had previously been used by Amadeus for house concerts. Trey was seated on a low stage at a desk with his open briefcase. The walls were covered with gold record plaques and photographs of Amadeus posing with many famous people. There was an enlarged picture of Amadeus with Queen Elizabeth II. Also, pushed against the wall were a piano, three guitars, and several music stands. The floor was covered with a MacDonald patterned plaid carpet.

The chairs were arranged in a semi-circle so all in attendance could see each other. As usual, Reverend MacDonald acted as host, leading Phyllida, Prudence, Vanessa, and Yuri to their chairs. Florence and her children were already seated. All were looking fatigued and emotionally drained. Fergus, Jr. sat beside his mother, who was urging him to silence, since he had already indulged in an alcoholic outburst during lunch.

Trey began reading as soon as all were seated. He confirmed that Florence would continue to live at the estate and home she legally co-owned with Amadeus and would receive two-thirds of their financial wealth. Amadeus bequeathed 200,000 pounds to Prudence with the remainder of his wealth to be divided equally among his children. He emphasized that Vanessa Silver should be included equally. The money was to be held in trust with quarterly payments. The estimated yearly income from cash and investments would be approximately 100,000 pounds per beneficiary. Amadeus' will emphasized his wish for each of his children's ability to do what they wanted, but not so much wealth that they could do nothing. Amadeus also stipulated that any dispute of the will could cause that person to receive nothing.

Yuri resisted the desire to pull out his phone and convert English pounds to American dollars. Prudence gasped as she realized

Amadeus' belated gift to her acknowledged their past relationship. Vanessa looked more amazed and confused than anything else. Fergus, Jr. remained silent with his mouth opening and closing as he struggled to stay silent.

Trey announced that he would meet individually with each recipient for all the proper data collection, signing of forms, and filing the official documents within a week. As the family left the room, they found a table set with glasses of sherry. Everyone took a glass and drank quickly as a covenant to Amadeus' final wishes.

Fiona drove everyone to the B&B in silence. The exhausted mourners went to their rooms for rest and contemplation of the day's life changing events.

Who Killed Amadeus?

The morning after the burial, Llewellyn had arranged a day trip to explore the sights of Skye with Prudence, Vanessa, and Yuri. Phyllida remained behind for a quiet time. She planned to find a bench with a sea view. She found what she was looking for approximately a thirty-minute walk from the B&B just past Portree High Street. Shortly after she sat with her hat pulled down and jacket collar zipped up against the wind, a group of pipe-smoking men, standing on the beach began talking. These grey bearded men were all wearing knitted sweaters and caps of undyed wool.

"You know, Amadeus was buried yesterday. His killer's still on the loose."

"Aye. Who do ye' think killed him? The old girlfriend d' nay seem the type for revenge killing. Why wait all these years? Her bairn all grown 'n all?"

Every word was carried by the wind to Phyllida's ears.

"Y' know Old Man MacQueen still holds a grudge from losing the family estate to Amadeus. He can be a vengeful bugger."

"Aye, Superintendent Jones should check it out."

"Aye, maybe he already has."

With the change of wind, Phyllida could hear nothing more of the conversation. She remained seated until the men left the beach. On her way back to the B&B, she stopped in at Portree Tea Shoppe for hot tea and soup. The more she thought, the more she felt the need to talk to Superintendent Jones. *I'm sure he knows local history, but I want to be sure he checked out the bad history between Amadeus and Old Man MacQueen. It's time to get this murder solved and return home!*

Superintendent Jones had planned an intense day of studying yesterday's video, covering the funeral and burial of Amadeus. The first interruption was a call from Superintendent Harold Green in London.

"Hey, Jones, how far along are you in finding Amadeus' murderer? Is the jilted old girlfriend guilty?"

"No, Prudence Silver and her friend, Phyllida Walker, are no longer prime suspects, in my opinion."

"Well, if you read the tattler rag Felicia Friday writes in, they're certainly prime suspects."

"What on earth has she written?"

"I hope you're sitting down. She suggests the women 'bumped Amadeus off so the bastard daughter, her words – not mine – could collect an inheritance.' She goes on to say, 'Superintendent Jones has become so friendly with the suspects that he's letting them get away with murder.'"

"Bloody Hell! That woman is an attention-seeking viper with no thought to who or what she hurts. I'm going over video of the funeral right now. Wait 'til you see the shenanigans she pulled to intrude herself into the funeral."

"I'll leave you to it. Keep me posted."

"Of course, I'm sending the video now for you to look over. More eyes, the better."

"Cheers, I'll check it out."

Phyllida was deep in thought as she walked slowly back to the B&B. *Do I call Superintendent Jones about the mention of "Old Man MacQueen" or relax and assume he knows what he's doing?*

Suddenly, four teens – two girls and two boys – formed a circle around her. "Hey, Miss, we could use some of your tourist money. How much you got in your satchel?"

Phyllida looked up at this motley group. "Well, let me see." She unzipped the satchel, reached in, and deftly removed her pepper spray.

"Bitch," they screamed, running away. With tearing eyes, the young thugs were screaming in pain.

A uniformed policewoman jumped out of an unmarked police car and came running. "Good job, Miss. If you're okay, I'll just catch that lot."

Phyllida nodded her head and saw the officer speak into her phone. A police car quickly blocked the rowdy group. The officers deftly searched and handcuffed the hooligans.

"Would you be kind enough to come to the station and give a statement, Miss?"

"I certainly will!" Phyllida spoke, slightly out of breath from the excitement "In fact, I was hoping to speak with Superintendent Jones."

"I'll see if Superintendent Jones is available."

On the short ride to the police headquarters, the officer called into the station. "There's a lady mugged by four juveniles coming in to give a statement. She's asking to speak with Superintendent Jones. What's your name, Miss?"

"Phyllida Walker. Superintendent Jones knows me."

As Phyllida walked into the station, Superintendent Jones was waiting in reception.

"This trip you and your friend arranged has so much unexpected drama. You should take your travel agent to task."

"I was deep in thought when those kids surrounded me. Thank God I carry pepper spray." Turning to the arresting officer, Phyllida continued, "those hooligans formed a circle around me and demanded money. As I reached into my satchel, I quickly pulled out the pepper spray as you can see, and I'm impressed at how quickly you came to my rescue. Thank you very much."

"If you're finished giving the sergeant your statement, come to my office."

"Certainly."

Superintendent Jones' office was small and cluttered. A heavy all-weather anorak hung on a coat tree with a black hard hat, labeled "Portree Police."

Phyllida came straight to the point. "I overheard some older, pipe-smoking men on the beach, discussing whether Old Man MacQueen might be the murderer. I was debating with myself whether to call you with the information or assume you had already considered this old man who lost the estate to Amadeus."

"I've considered Angus MacQueen, but I haven't visited him yet. I will in the next day or so. Right now, I'm arranging a ride for you back to the B&B. I'm very sorry you were attacked by those neds. You certainly impressed them with your self-defense skills. They won't try mugging any other white-haired tourists any time soon. Well done!"

"What are neds if you don't mind me asking? I'm behind on UK slang."

"Non educated delinquents, which is exactly why they were running on the streets. Here's your ride. Be alert when walking around. Even Portree has some unsavory elements."

"I can't thank you enough, Superintendent."

The Search is On

Phyllida couldn't get the thought of Old Man MacQueen out of her head. She pulled out her iPad and searched for Angus MacQueen, Skye, Scotland. She read about the MacQueens' long history on Skye, including a brief mention of a dilapidated estate won in a poker game by Amadeus. *So, there's truth in the rumor.*

Suddenly the noise of Prudence, Vanessa, and Yuri returning had her opening the adjoining door to Prudence's room.

"We've brought early supper. Llewellyn took us on a wonderful drive around Skye, and then we stopped for some great fish and chips."

"I can smell the malt vinegar from here. I love fish and chips."

"How did your day go? Did you find a good place to meditate?"

"My meditation spot was wonderful. I overheard interesting gossip from some older men before the wind changed. During my walk back, I was held up by four young hooligans who wanted my money. What they got instead was pepper spray. Luckily for me, a police patrol was passing. I gave a statement at the station and talked with Superintendent Jones."

"Oh my God!" Vanessa exclaimed after hearing about the mugging.

"You need someone with you when you go out. Yuri or I will come with you on the next outing."

"My dears, Pru and I took a self-defense course together. The pepper spray came to the rescue. Now, help me research the senior Angus MacQueen. What does he look like? Was he in London for Amadeus' concert? Yuri and Vanessa are so much cleverer with the internet than I am. Wonder if the local library has some helpful information that I can access without making waves."

Phyllida was sitting yoga-style on her bed in her purple paisley pants. Everyone was munching on fish and chips as they researched.

"I found a picture," Yuri announced as he showed his discovery to Phyllida. "Wonder how old this photo is?"

Phyllida leaned over to see better. "Heavens, he looks like all the other grizzled old men on Skye. Don't men shave anymore? Sorry, Yuri, you're forgiven." She noticed the three-day blond stubble. "It must be a relief not to shave for a few days."

It seems that Superintendent Jones was struggling with similar questions. *I can't wait any longer to interview Florence MacCann and William. I need to find out more about the fans and friends in the dressing room. Dammit! London needs to get me copies of their interviews. Really difficult to have the scene of the crime so far away from the people involved.*

Wait a minute – someone should investigate Felicia Friday. She was at the concert and apparently knew where the dressing room was located. I think I'm going to enjoy this. We'll have her in an interview room with my sergeant as witness and recordings to verify the specifics. Let her make what she will about that. For now, I'll get on with interviewing Florence and William.

Reverend MacDonald, who was helping Florence in handling much of Amadeus' business, answered the phone. They had been working on the tough job of official death notifications. Amadeus was on the board of a few local organizations. They needed to cancel credit cards. Bank accounts had to be put in Florence's name. Each notification felt like reliving Amadeus' death. The call from Superintendent Jones was more a relief than an annoyance.

"Good day to you, Reverend. Sorry to interrupt, but it's time I interviewed Florence and William. I need specifics about Amadeus' visitors to his dressing room at the Palladium."

"Can William and Florence be interviewed here?"

"Yes, I can do the interviews at the estate. My sergeant will accompany me. I need to interview each of them separately, of course."

"Of course. We'll be ready this afternoon." Florence had been listening on the extension.

Jones and Sergeant McCloud drove to the Amadeus estate within 45 minutes of the phone call. William directed them to park nearest the front door and showed them inside. The Reverend MacDonald, continuing to act as host, led them to a small office with a clear desktop and amazingly comfortable padded chairs. *We could get used to these chairs,* Jones mused.

"I would like to interview you first, Florence." Jones adjusted his chair to face her with the recording device resting on the desk. "How many people from Skye were in and out of the dressing room during Amadeus' rehearsals and performance?"

"Most of the musicians and his manager were there. Most musicians live in the area, so they're available to rehearse. His manager is based in London. He was in and out of the Palladium during the four days of rehearsals and present for the performance."

"Did anyone in the dressing room adjust the heater? Too hot or too cold?"

"I don't think I even noticed a heater in the room. It was stuffy when fans and musicians gathered to celebrate with champagne after the concert. Everyone was elated at the wonderful reception. The concert went brilliantly. Amadeus was thrilled and in a happy celebratory mood. I could see he would continue drinking throughout the night. Now, I'm so sorry I didn't stay with him." Florence gasped as she spoke, tears coming down her cheeks. "I trusted William to stay with Amadeus. William nearly died too!"

"We can take a break if you need." Superintendent Jones motioned for Sergeant McCloud to get Florence a glass of water. Florence sipped.

"I'll continue. I want this murderer caught as much as you do. I thought Amadeus and I would have so much more time together. Cherish the time with your wife, Marcus. We never know what will interrupt our happy lives."

Sergeant McCloud, seated beside Florence, moved the box of tissues closer.

"Have there been any threats or expressions of hostility toward Amadeus recently?"

"There were always weirdos who said nasty things. Amadeus had a robust and loud personality, and he could be overwhelming at times. Someone was always getting offended."

"Did Amadeus socialize with Angus MacQueen after winning your estate from him? Did Angus ever get over it?"

"This estate was a rundown mess. It's taken years and buckets of money to get it to its present condition. MacQueen laughed about it. It saved him from bleeding more money and property taxes. Mind you, he had a point. This estate is very costly to maintain, as I am learning."

"Florence, do you think Angus MacQueen may have been at the Palladium before or during Amadeus' concert?"

"I seriously doubt it. He can't stand Amadeus' style of music. Also, he's severely crippled with arthritis."

"This is helpful, Florence. Thanks so much. Can someone let William know I'm ready for him now."

William was sitting on a bench in the garden, waiting to be called. He smiled pleasantly; however, a map of stress lines showed on his forehead. He was dressed in khaki slacks and a navy knit polo shirt with a Ralph Lauren logo.

"Have a seat, William. Remind me of your surname, please."

"My last name is McCloud, Sir."

"Are you related to the McClouds of Skye? I don't remember you around when I was younger."

"My family goes back several generations on Skye. My grandfather moved to London where I grew up, but I visited Skye every year as a child. Actually, Amadeus and I are distant cousins."

"I see. When did you start working for Amadeus?"

"I was a fledgling singer, looking for work. Amadeus was starting to get famous and hired me. Originally, I was a chauffeur and helped keep the music room and business desk organized. Twenty-five years later and here I am. Did a bit of everything to assist Amadeus and now Florence. I am a Jeeves to Amadeus' Bertie Wooster."

With a laugh, Superintendent Jones continued, "My wife and children are very fond of the old Jeeves and Wooster program on the telly; however, I need you to be a bit more specific."

"I maintained Amadeus' clothes and made sure his tartans

were cleaned, pressed and ready to wear. I kept up with fashion and made sure he was always properly dressed. I kept the diary for all Amadeus' appointments – whether medical, business, or social. I kept credit cards and cash to purchase anything Amadeus decided to buy. I caddied his golf games. I made all his reservations. I also serve Florence and young Malcolm. I drive young Malcolm to school and social events. I pick up prescriptions for Florence, drive her to friends or card games where there will be drinking. I also provide advice on fashion choices."

"You sound like a very valuable member of the household."

"I like to think so."

"Were you as helpful to Amadeus in London as you were at home?"

"I was the go-between for Amadeus, the Palladium, and his manager. I was the major doorkeeper to let the right persons in and keep the undesirables out."

"What about the heater? Did you or anyone else adjust it?"

"When we first arrived in the dressing room, the door had been closed and there was a metallic, stale odor. I complained. The Palladium management stated the heater had recently been serviced. I tried to keep the door or window open. I think when the last people left after the celebration, someone must have closed the window and door to make us more comfortable. We were both drunk with good French Champagne. This was one of the few times I let my guard down because the concert was over. Amadeus was asleep in a reclining chair, and I was on a sofa. I have a vague memory of someone draping a blanket over each of us and closing both the window and door."

"This is the most detailed information I've received to date, William. Can you give me a list of people in the dressing room?"

"All the musicians, the manager, George Johns, Florence, a few fans from the original fan club. Fan club people were mostly elderly women, expressing their love for Amadeus with gorgeous flower arrangements, his favorite foods – especially fresh smoked salmon with cream cheese tea sandwiches, chocolate covered strawberries, and several bottles of Dom Perignon. I monitored the door and kept unknown persons and media out."

"Has Angus MacQueen ever attended an Amadeus concert or attempted to come backstage?"

"Not to my knowledge. Old Man MacQueen and Amadeus seldom socialized after the famous poker game. There was a rumor that MacQueen lost on purpose to avoid paying taxes."

"Are you aware of the reporter, Felicia Friday? She appears to have been taking a real interest in Amadeus."

"I've seen her less-than-complimentary television presentations and the newspaper articles that imply that Prudence Silver was somehow involved in Amadeus' death. I get the feeling she tried to make big news from scant knowledge."

"I suspect you're correct. Who were the last people leaving the dressing room? The ones who spread blankets and closed the door?"

"I have racked my brain trying to remember this. I get a fuzzy image of a man in the grey coat worn by stagehands."

"You're sure it was a man? Any details, such as tall or short, fat or thin?"

"I really am struggling to remember, Superintendent. Amadeus' death is horrible. He was a true friend. I miss him terribly."

"My condolences, William. Please contact me if there's anything else you can remember."

Superintendent Jones returned to the police station with his head spinning. *Bloody hell! William saw someone closing the door and windows. Did this person know he was creating a death trap, or did he finish what he had started?*

It was late afternoon when Superintendent Jones called his London contact, Superintendent Harold Green. "Did you know that William McCloud vaguely remembers seeing someone close the window and door at the Palladium, which resulted in the CO poisoning?"

"Did he, indeed? He was pretty fuzzy when we interviewed him just after the death. Who did he see?"

"He was too drunk and sleepy to identify the person. He

remembers the grey Palladium coat used by all the stagehands."

"Palladium stagehands all denied seeing anything. I'll get right onto questioning them again. Any description to help narrow the search?"

"Alas, no. Let me know what you discover as soon as possible. Thanks, Hal."

"It's going to take a few days. There are about 15 people to interview. Glad you called. Higher-ups are anxious to get this murder solved. All the gossip from that rag Felicia Friday works for is like throwing firecrackers into a crowd. Makes us all jump for no good reason."

Digging Deeper

Phyllida, Prudence, Vanessa, and Yuri were finishing a late breakfast at the B&B.

"Darlings," Phyllida lowered her teacup as she began to speak. "I think we should all check Facebook to find the date when all the snarky innuendos about Amadeus began. This may give us a clue about who the writer is and why someone was angry enough to murder Amadeus. By the way, Superintendent Jones has determined that Felicia Friday did not make these remarks in Facebook directed at Prudence. It's interesting that this person knew about Prudence and Vanessa and felt vindictive towards Amadeus."

"What a good idea to check, Philly. I'll start this morning," Prudence replied.

"We'll check as soon as we return from our lesson with the Scottish Country Dance Master. Mattias Jones is immensely proud of his dance group. He's gifted us with new ballet-style ghillies with extreme impact protection. It's amazing that Superintendent Jones and his identical twin are in such different professions." Yuri stood up and held the chair for Vanessa. They smiled at Prudence and Phyllida as they left the room holding hands.

"Have a good time, darlings," Prudence called.

Phyllida returned to her room. She was listening to a Deepak Chopra meditation on finding gratitude during challenging times. Currently, she was reading articles on women taking their power back in an Oprah Winfrey *O Magazine* she found in the B&B's small assortment of reading material. Since the mugging, she had lost a desire to take long walks alone.

Felicia Friday was making the Hare and Hound Pub a regular stop since learning that Vanessa and Yuri were planning to attend the next dance. She sat on a barstool, sipping a pint of ale, waiting for the dancers to arrive at 15:00. *Blimey, my wait paid off. Here come the dancers with – am I seeing right? With Superintendent Jones and another Scot in a kilt!*

The Barman called out, "Hey, Jonesy, shall I bring a pitcher of lager to the back room?"

"Great idea. Oh, two shandies as well."

Royal Scottish Country Dancing

Mattias Jones smiled at Yuri and Vanessa as he introduced his dancing colleague. "Allow me to present Mr. Iain Roberts, the famous Scottish Country Dance instructor and deviser." With a wave of his arm, he continued, "Iain, Yuri Chermovsky and Vanessa Silver are dancers with the San Francisco Ballet. They gave me tracings of their feet, and I've purchased ghillies so they can join us for this Saturday's dance."

Yuri and Vanessa immediately put on the black ballet style shoes and laced them. They began to move and walk around the room. "We spend considerable time breaking in dancing shoes. They work well for me." Vanessa executed a grand high kick and twirl.

"Me as well," Yuri added.

With a serious expression, Yuri asked Mattias, "Tell me how you and your twin chose such different ways of life, if that's not too personal."

"'Tis so well known locally that there's no secret. While Marcus began his training in the police service, I joined the army and was sent to Bosnia. I sustained a serious injury to my left shoulder and arm, my dominant side, which left me retired with a pension. M'wife, Josie, led me to Scottish Country Dancing to get me out of a serious depression. In time, I became the local leader and instructor. I also serve on a Skye Police Commission and review my own brother's reports. Believe you me, I am strict with Marcus' reports."

Iain put on his ghillies and inserted a CD for some dance music. "Now, let me show you some steps. This music is for a strathspey." Iain began nimbly dancing across the room. He was followed by Yuri and Vanessa, mirroring his moves. "Grand! Now let me quicken the pace with a jig." Again, his pupils were quickly following him. "I brought diagrams of the dances we'll be doing this Saturday."

"Yuri and I are going to enjoy this!" Dancing energized Vanessa, and Yuri smiled at her enthusiasm. Such a relief from her worry about her mother being falsely accused of murder.

After some practice, it was obvious that Yuri and Vanessa would add sparkle and grace to Saturday's dance. All the local dancers arrived an hour later to practice with their American guests. It was exciting to see the way professional dancers added polish and style to the choreography.

"You're all looking marvelous!" Mattias cheered. "Do we have the proper dress and kilt for our talented guests?"

"It's all in hand, dear," Josie assured her husband. "We're all going to look gorgeous on Saturday. Yuri and Vanessa, I'll drive you to the tailors to be measured."

"Oh, we'll pay for the costumes. They'll be a great souvenir from Skye."

"Mattias and I really insist. This will be our gift for the pleasure of your dancing with us."

Felicia Friday had been nursing a pint of Skye Gold Ale as she waited for the group to come out of the back room. She was able to get a clear shot of Mattias with an arm over Yuri's shoulder and a second shot of Vanessa with her ghillies draped over her shoulder. *I can hardly wait to photograph the Saturday dance. It'll be a great piece for my paper. Maybe I'll get a raise! Maybe I'll title my story, "The Dancing Policeman."*

Preparations for the coming Scottish Dance took everyone's mind off the strain of the unsolved murder.

The tailor had their kilts ready to try on by Thursday. "I took the liberty of choosing the MacPhail plaid for Sir's kilt and the inset of plaid on Madam's dress. Amadeus' maternal grandfather was a MacPhail. I should know. Amadeus was my second cousin." The tall slender man expertly placed the kilt belt, sporran, and matching plaid on the kilt hose before taking a photograph. Vanessa's dress was black with a fitted bodice and a flared trumpet skirt. A MacPhail plaid sash completed her outfit. Four inverted pleats in the skirt showed the MacPhail plaid as she twirled. Vanessa playfully held the skirt out to show the plaid as her photo was taken.

The next days passed quickly for Yuri and Vanessa. They cleared a space in their room to practice the dances, and they took leisurely walks around Portree with Phyllida and Prudence before dinner.

Phyllida diligently coordinated the dates of Facebook posts to Vanessa and Prudence, looking for a pattern. She noted these posts with the name "Anonymous" began in April and were posted to both women on the same days. *I'm convinced these snarky postings are from one person. I wonder what occurred with Amadeus that might trigger some long-held grudge? I'll have to phone Superintendent Jones since I don't feel free to call Florence. Also, I might alert a guilty party in the Amadeus household.*

Superintendent Jones was feeling frustrated with the Amadeus case. He had not heard from Green, his colleague in London, who was interviewing the Palladium stagehands for a second time. He found these lags in communication an ongoing problem. The call from Phyllida was welcome. "Hello, Mrs. Walker, what can I do for you?"

"Good afternoon, Superintendent. I've made a list of Facebook posts to Prudence and Vanessa with snarky comments about their relationship to Amadeus. They began in early April and both women were contacted on the same days. What do you know about Amadeus' life that would stir up old grudges?"

"You're a good detective. I appreciate your work, Mrs. Walker."

"Please call me Phyllida. No need for formalities."

"I'll check my notes and get back to you." Superintendent Jones sighed heavily after he finished his call with Phyllida. *It's embarrassing when the suspects are trying to help me solve this murder! Just in case she has a point, I'll call William and ask for Amadeus' diary. There's been so much going on I've neglected to check it until now.*

"Hello, William, how are you today? Are you and the MacCann family coping better with your grieving?"

"You know, I believe it's getting better for me, at least. Florence is overwhelmed with business matters that leave her little time to grieve, except for private moments early in the morning and late at night."

"I'm glad to hear it's improving for you. By the way, do you have Amadeus' diary? I need to read it. Will it be necessary to get a warrant? ... No, I didn't think so. What months does it cover? ... January to his death will do. I'll come by today to collect it. I'm also very interested in what was happening in March and April that might have awakened old grudges."

"No mystery there, Superintendent. Amadeus was contacting all past and present performers who had appeared with him. Some of the people go back more than thirty years."

"Good to know. I would also like to interview you and Florence again about life with Amadeus in March and April. Were there any incidents that might have stirred old grudges or hard feelings?"

"Let me just check that Florence is available." Jones could hear William walking, then the muffled sounds of a female voice. "Yes, Sir, Florence will expect you at 1:30."

Superintendent Jones leaned back in his chair with feet on the desk for a good think. *Leave it to Phyllida to wake me up to a new line of questioning.*

Let's Dance

"Oh, Philly, you look really nice. It's great to have an outing that's simply for pleasure. Yuri and Vanessa look magnificent in their Scottish Dancing costumes! Let's take a group picture over here by the fireplace." Prudence was wearing grey slacks with a turquoise silk shirt and matching sweater. Phyllida was wearing black slacks with a bright purple blouse and black tweed sweater. The group began taking pictures with their phones.

"Mattias is just outside, double parked, in the van he borrowed from Marcus." Yuri held the door as they walked to the waiting van.

"What a glorious group you make! Iain is already at the pub to set up the video, and my wife is finishing the decorations. She's the person behind the scenes who keeps this group running smoothly with her careful attention to detail. The pub has set up a buffet with food and drink."

Felicia Friday chose a place at the end of the bar. The doors to the back room were completely open, allowing a full view of the dancing. *This is going to be my best story yet! I already have the story line running through my head. I think my new plaid cap with my hair tucked up will disguise me. Regardless, I have every right to sit here and enjoy the dancing.*

As Mattias and his guests walked into the Hare and Hound Pub, they met several early arriving Scottish dancers. The musicians were tuning their instruments as Yuri and Vanessa joined the group of dancers.

Josie led Phyllida and Prudence to a back table. "I've chosen this spot so you can watch Vanessa and Yuri. I took the liberty of ordering the Pub's baked chicken with potatoes and vegetables for you. It's one of my favorite dishes here."

Prudence and Phyllida sat facing the dancers. Mattias brought them two pints of Skye Gold Ale. "Local ale is on the house, but the dancers won't eat until intermission."

"This is such a lovely way to spend a Saturday. Finally, we get to see the local culture." Prudence took a sip of ale as she watched the dancers warm up.

At an adjacent table, an older couple was watching the dancers. "Look, dear. They must be the ballet dancers from America. Wow, she just put her leg over the chair. She looks like a swan with her head on her knee. She looks so much like Llewellyn MacCann it's startling. Wonder how the half-sisters feel about their strong resemblance?" The wife rested her hand on her husband's arm as she spoke.

"This small island certainly allows rumors to spread like wildfire," Phyllida whispered to Prudence.

The clang of a spoon on an ale pitcher brought quiet. Iain Roberts looked handsome in his watch plaid kilt, white shirt, and narrow black tie.

"We have guest dancers from the San Francisco Ballet joining us this evening. Please introduce yourselves to Vanessa Silver and Yuri Chermovsky. Let's warm up by walking in a circle." The dancers exercised various muscle groups, rolling shoulders, elbows, and hands. Then they continued the circle as the dance master called different steps: "on your toes, skip-change, pas de Basque, slip step in second position moving sideways, traveling step, side to side."

"Please take partners for the first dance." The musicians tuned for the beginning dance as partners joined their sets of six. The dancing was graceful and complex. Some newer dancers scrambled to stay in step or ran to catch up. The circle with Yuri and Vanessa never missed a step as they elegantly performed a beautiful reel, followed by a strathspey and then two energetic jigs.

After an hour of dancing, the break allowed Yuri and Vanessa to get snacks from the buffet. They quenched their thirst with ginger beer before joining Prudence and Phyllida. Prudence took Vanessa's hand and smiled across at Yuri.

"I don't often get to see you dance this close. I'm always inspired by your talent and grace. How do memorize the dances so quickly?"

"Thanks, Mother. Choreography is a language we speak easily, and we had a practice session with the local dancers." Vanessa drank her ginger beer and bit into Stilton cheese on a thin French baguette.

Mattias was sitting with his wife and another couple as Felicia Friday caught a picture of him heartily laughing and holding a turkey leg. She had several pictures of him dancing. She was headlining her article, "The Dancing Detective."

In her enthusiasm, she finished her pint of ale and ordered another. *At times like this, I really love my job.*

The dancing began with Felicia happily photographing Mattias Jones – his set was closest to her. *Too bad Prudence and Phyllida are hidden at the back of the room. I got some wonderful shots of Vanessa Silver as she warmed up. I wish she and Yuri were closer for some dancing shots. I understand there's a last waltz – a great opportunity to get a couple of glamour shots of the American professionals.*

Oh, blimey! I'm feeling awful. Where's my blood sugar test kit? Felicia got out the equipment to stick her finger and the tape to test her sugar level. She was so trembly that the kit spilled onto the bar in front of her as the barman leaned over to take a good look. He quickly removed her ale.

"What's this, lass? Are you diabetic? No more ale for you. Hey, Doc Hanratty, come over and check this woman."

As Felicia turned to look behind her, she toppled off the barstool with a tremendous crash. *Oh, bloody hell! Superintendent Jones will be onto me.*

The noise caused everyone to stare in her direction. Prudence and Phyllida looked toward the bar and saw Felicia Friday on the floor.

"Don't tell me that awful reporter needs first aid again! Thank God we don't need to come to the rescue this time," grumbled Phyllida. "Lucky for her! I'd be tempted to kick her in the butt instead of injecting insulin."

"I thought Superintendent Jones told her to quit following us."

Prudence leaned to see better as she spoke. "Fortunate for her a doctor seems to be handy. Hope she doesn't think that plaid cap is a disguise."

Felicia still sat on the floor as the doctor expertly pricked her finger and touched it to the strip. "Your blood sugar has dropped. She needs some orange juice and maybe some meat or cheese on crackers," Dr. Hanratty shouted to the bartender.

Felicia stood up weakly and returned to the barstool. "I'll be fine in just a minute. Then I'll drive back to my hotel."

"Oh, no, lass." The barman expertly grabbed the car keys. "Taxi for you tonight. You can collect your car tomorrow. The car park is safe enough for overnight. You are in the car park, aren't you?"

Felicia weakly nodded her head as a waitress led her outside to wait for the taxi.

"I'll just wait with you, so the driver understands you're ill and not drunk. You should be more careful as a diabetic."

"You're right, of course. Here's the taxi now. Thank you for your trouble."

"No bother. I'll just have a smoke before going back in."

Back at her hotel, Felicia drank more orange juice and ate the additional cheese and bread the barman gave her. *Damn, I wanted to stay for the end of the dancing. I do have plenty to write, though. If I send my story by 3 a.m., I'll be fine.*

The Dancing Detective

Felicia speedily typed on her laptop. She kept her article short to make the deadline and include the photographs, which she knew her readers would love.

The Dancing Detective

Since the murder of Amadeus by carbon monoxide poisoning in a dressing room at the Palladium, I have followed this great entertainer to his funeral in his family home on Skye. From my balcony seat in row DD13 at his last performance at the Palladium, I identified Amadeus' former lover and mother of his love child, Prudence Silver, accompanied by her longtime friend, Phyllida Walker. They attended the final performance of Amadeus at the Palladium and exited down back stairs past Amadeus' dressing room. Did they enter the room and manipulate the furnace so that it emitted carbon monoxide that killed Amadeus? I don't know.

Superintendent Marcus Jones, in Portree, Skye, has the duty of overseeing the two murder suspects. Did the women "just so happen" to be in Skye in time to attend the funeral of Amadeus? Even though they are required to remain in Portree, they are currently living comfortably in a local B & B. Superintendent Jones seems to have more of a social oversight over the two women, including dining out with his family.

In fact, there appears to be a case of the fox guarding the chicken coop. The superintendent has a love of Scottish dancing that he's incorporated into his police duties. The daughter of Amadeus and Prudence Silver, Vanessa Silver, has joined her mother on Skye along with her husband, Yuri Chermovsky – they are both members of the San Francisco Ballet. On Saturday last, they danced with Jones' Scottish

Dance Group at Hare and Hound Pub in Portree. Prudence Silver and Phyllida Walker enjoyed a pub dinner and drank Skye Gold Ale while watching the dancing. You could say the Superintendent Inspector kept the women under observation all the while – note the pictures below showing Jones both expertly dancing and, during a break, enjoying a good laugh and turkey leg. Also, note the beautiful Vanessa Silver preparing to dance. She has a strong resemblance to her half-sister, Amadeus' legitimate daughter, Llewellyn MacCann, by his wife, Florence MacCann.

Who killed Amadeus? What is Superintendent Marcus Jones doing to determine if Prudence Silver and Phyllida Walker are white-haired murderers? If the women are innocent, why are they required to remain on Skye?

This is Felicia Friday, keeping you posted from Portree, Skye.

Felicia proofread her article three times before pushing the send key. She then brushed her teeth, removed her make-up, lay down on her bed, and fell into a deep sleep. At noon, she got up and jumped into jeans and rushed to the front desk to collect the current copy of *the London Inquirer*. She began reading her article as she walked along the corridor to her room.

Great! The column made the first page. The photographs are wonderful. I can hardly wait for Superintendent Jones to react. Wish I could see his face. I need to go to the dining room and eat. I'm feeling a bit shaky.

Felicia ordered an herb omelet and green salad to accommodate her diabetes diet. *I'll take a long walk to get my required exercise this afternoon.* Her cell phone began ringing. "Hello, Guv, hope you enjoyed the story I sent."

"Not nearly as much as the town of Portree and the Jones twins. You might want to get a copy of the *Portree Gazette*." Chief Editor, Roland Ogilvy growled his orders. "Read the story; then call me back."

"Twins! What twins?" Felicia was totally confused.

"Read the local rag! Then call me back!" He hung up before Felicia could answer.

Felicia left the remains of her meal and went to the paper stand by the front desk. She bought the last copy of the *Portree Gazette*. The frontpage featured Superintendent Jones standing beside his identical twin, Mattias Jones. Felicia returned to her room to read the article.

Portree's Jones Twins Confuse London Reporter

It seems our London reporter, Felicia Friday, has confused wounded army veteran, Mattias Jones for his twin, Superintendent Detective Marcus Jones of the Portree local constabulary. Could it be due to the diabetic episode Saturday night that caused her to fall off her barstool? Seems she believed Marcus Jones was dancing while he should be solving the murder of Amadeus. Marcus was in London, consulting with his counterpart, Superintendent Green. Green has interviewed the stagehands at the Palladium for the second time, searching for the guilty party who may have sabotaged the heater.

Informed sources report that Amadeus and many fans were in the throes of celebrating as the white-haired women suspects named by Friday exited the Palladium and arrived back at their hotel. Methinks Friday should leave the detective work to Marcus Jones. She obviously isn't very good at it.

Felicia let out a loud scream as she threw a glass that shattered on the wall. A knock on her door forced her to straighten up, appearing normal as she answered.

A cleaner looked concerned as she asked, "Is everything alright, Madam?"

"Sorry, I just got some disturbing news." Felicia was fighting back tears as she spoke.

"Does your room need cleaning?"

"No, thank you. There's no problem."

Felicia carefully cleaned up the broken glass, cutting a finger, which triggered the tears she had been holding back.

The cell phone rang as she was hiccupping the last of her tears. She steeled herself as she answered. "Hello, Guv. I had no idea Superintendent Jones was an identical twin. I'm really sorry."

"You bloody well should be sorry. What's this about diabetes? Does it make you doolally?"

"No, I have type 2 diabetes, easily controlled with food and exercise. I just happened to go too long without eating at the Hare and Hound."

"So you say. I want you back in London in my office tomorrow to discuss a few things."

"But Sir, I can write a retraction and provide some more intimate information about Vanessa Silver and her mother, Prudence, along with Phyllida Walker."

"No, you've already written some pretty damning stuff. The paper doesn't want a lawsuit. Have your arse in my office tomorrow!" Again, Roland Ogilvy hung up before she could reply.

Oh God! How could things go so wrong? Damn Superintendent Jones and his twin! Damn Prudence Silver and Phyllida Walker! Damn Amadeus – I'm glad he's dead!

Called Back to London

Felicia slowly began packing for her return to London as she contemplated a way to save her reputation and her job. She traveled to the airport for a flight to London in a hired car driven by Superintendent Marcus Jones' wife. Felicia wore sunglasses in the foggy afternoon to hide her red-rimmed eyes. Superintendent Jones and all Portree rejoiced at her departure. Jones took copies of the *London Inquirer* and the *Portree Gazette* to present to Prudence and Phyllida as souvenirs.

Felicia lived in a small apartment on Jermyn Street in the Piccadilly Circus area of London. Her apartment smelled stale and damp. She turned on her wall heater as she unpacked and prepared a suit for meeting with her boss tomorrow. *Hopefully, my red suit will show Ogilvy I'm a professional reporter ready for action.*

The London morning was dripping with fog and rain. Felicia entered her workspace, carrying a large paper cup of vending machine coffee. Before she could take a sip, Roland Ogilvy was standing beside her.

"My office, please, Ms. Friday." His formality felt intimidating.

"Sir." Felicia clasped her hands around her cup to avoid any shaking as she followed Ogilvy into his office. She felt tiny in the chair across from the big desk.

"I've spoken to the NHS nurse on duty here, and you will start each day with a pin prick to measure your blood sugar. I have a local assignment for you. Lady Jane Ames is presenting some prize orchids to the Princess of Wales House in Kew Gardens. I want some beautiful pictures and a lovely story, paying tribute to Lady Jane Ames and her dear friend, the late Princess Diana. If the story is good enough, I'll put it in the Sunday Society Section."

Felicia gulped her helpless dismay as she uttered, "Sir."

"By the way, Lady Jane Ames is a personal friend of our paper's owner. Don't make waves. All our competitors are having a good laugh over your Amadeus story."

"Which photographer will accompany me?"

"You'll take your own bloody pictures just as you did in Portree! Again, no extravagant claims!"

Felicia left the office feeling sick. *Bloody hell, I need to eat before I see the nurse. I'm reduced to a flower show. This is humiliating.*

Having quickly choked down a vending machine cheese sandwich, Felicia dutifully appeared at the nurse's office. The nurse was a cheerful woman with salt and pepper hair. "Hello, dear. I hear you're adjusting to your recent diagnosis of diabetes. This will only sting for a moment." She expertly pricked the middle finger and placed a blood drop on a test strip, which she put in a meter to measure the blood glucose. "There, looking good, 100 ml. Remember to eat a little something every three hours. Good to carry a cheese stick in case of emergencies."

"Certainly, Nurse Franklin." Felicia thought her two Kit Kat bars would have to do.

Indulging in a taxi helped Felicia arrive at Kew Gardens Princess of Wales House in good time. She planned to take the Tube home afterwards to save money. A young woman met her at the orchid display. "May I see your invitation, Madam?"

"I'm the reporter assigned to cover today's event." Felicia quickly showed her reporter's identification card.

Luckily, the young woman accepted this as sufficient for entry. "Lady Jane will be glad to share her love of orchids, along with a few stories of her great friendship with the late Princess Diana. Have you and Lady Jane met?"

"No, but I've admired her for ages," Felicia lied.

"Wonderful! Mummy, this reporter is going to cover your presentation. Remind me of your name."

"I'm Felicia Friday. So pleased to meet you, Lady Jane." Felicia presented her right hand. Lady Jane offered her damp, limp hand. Felicia resisted cringing and smiled bravely.

"I didn't realize the paper was covering this afternoon's event. How lovely. Would you like some tea? We have about forty-five minutes before the presentation. My gardener is bringing the orchids in his truck. Felicity, darling, go help Jerome with the orchids. Oh, Ms. Friday, you will see some extraordinary plants!"

Felicia dutifully photographed each of the ten plants. She would look up orchids on the internet to learn what was so extraordinary.

Lady Jane was extremely fussy about how the plants were placed on the various height tables. "These gorgeous darlings must be allowed to display their individual beauty." Jerome moved the plants several times before Lady Jane was satisfied.

Felicia sat on a bench, waiting to take a photograph of the final placement. *Lord, this is tedious. My feet are killing me. I shouldn't have worn heels. With this picture, I can go straight home and turn in my story from my laptop.*

A slight ring of a teaspoon on a teacup gained the attention of 20 expensively dressed women, wearing necklaces of giant pearls or other precious jewels and even larger diamond rings, as they turned to face Lady Jane at the microphone.

"Let's take this moment to pay homage to my dear friend, Princess Diana. I am sure she would have loved these magnificent orchids from Africa, developed in my own greenhouse with the assistance of my gardener, Jerome. Please take a bow, Jerome." A smattering of polite applause completed the presentation.

With a final photograph of Lady Jane beside her display, Felicia completed her assignment. After a ten-minute walk with aching feet, Felicia reached the Tube station. Luckily, she was traveling in the opposite direction from rush hour and got a seat. Another fifteen-minute walk past Tesco's and up a short flight of stairs took her to her first floor flat.

Her feet throbbed from the abuse of the long walk in heels. She kicked the offending shoes into her closet and put on fleece-lined clogs. Sitting on her bed, she allowed herself to rest her head on a pillow for a moment. Two hours later, she was awakened by terrible nausea and an alarm blaring. A knock on her door forced her to get up.

At the door, the landlord, who lived in the top floor flat was yelling, "Everyone out! The carbon monoxide detector has gone off! I have no idea where the carbon monoxide is coming from. I've called the fire brigade."

As Felicia stood outside in fresh air with her neighbors, she had a terrible feeling that this was not a coincidence. *Oh God, I've been targeted. I need to call the police!*

Felicia sat in the open ambulance with a blanket wrapped around her as she breathed oxygen. "I'm a reporter, I've been writing about the Amadeus death. I think this may be the same person. Was my heater interfered with?"

"It certainly was. When did you last use this heater?"

"Last night and it didn't make me sick."

Investigation in Piccadilly Circus, London

A fire brigade responder turned off the heater, then adjusted it. One fireman informed his captain, "Someone physically moved the ballast so the air intake valve was partially obstructed. Right away, I could see the flame was flickering and not the desired blue."

The fire captain turned to Felicia, "How fortunate you were."

"I also have diabetes and feel a bit shaky." Felicia entered her apartment to grab some clothes, her laptop, and some notes in a large fabric satchel. She took the allowed five minutes with a fireman accompanying her. After she stepped outside, she said, "Just let me call my boss."

Felicia was trembling as she spoke to Roland Ogilvy. "Guv, the strangest thing! I've been poisoned by carbon monoxide. Someone jimmied my wall heater today while I was out. I'm on the way to hospital, but I can begin writing my story. I plan to stay in a hotel overnight; the Regency Hotel is near my flat."

"Bloody hell! Do you think this is related to the Amadeus poisoning?"

"I really do, Sir."

"I'm calling the police right now. Just get well. We'll cover the hotel for a week."

"Thank you so much, Guv. I'll get right on this story."

The hospital visit took two hours. Felicia drank orange juice and nibbled on the cheese and crackers she still had after a nurse measured her blood sugar. She took a taxi to the Regency where her room was booked and ready for check-in. As she entered the room, she was amazed at how relieved she felt to be safe. *Since the boss is covering expenses, I can order a nice dinner from room service. I'll have the special roast beef dinner.*

As she uploaded her orchid photos, she googled African orchids and copied Wikipedia almost verbatim. Her pictures, including Lady Jane Ames, completed the photo exhibit. After a diligent search, Felicia could find no mention of Lady Jane associated with Princess Diana. *I'll resist the temptation to suggest that Lady Jane was exaggerating this friendship. I'll just write something soppy to please my boss.*

Just as she finished a hot shower and was preparing to watch the telly in bed, the phone rang. "Ms. Friday, this is Superintendent Harold Green of Scotland Yard. I'm working on the Amadeus case. I understand you experienced a nasty carbon monoxide poisoning."

"Yes, Sir, I certainly did. My gas wall heater worked fine last night. When I returned from an assignment today, it nearly killed me. Thank God my landlord had installed a carbon monoxide detector."

"That certainly was fortunate. I suspect this is related to the Amadeus death and your recent article from Skye."

"I agree, Superintendent. How can I help you?"

"We need to do a forensic examination of your apartment. How much was the heater handled?"

"The fire brigade turned off the heater and removed the front panel. I was told the air intake valve was partially blocked; one of the brigade returned the heating unit half an inch, which placed the valve correctly and allowed proper air intake. I was instructed not to use the heater until it's evaluated by Health and Safety. I'm staying at the Regency all week. I'll give you my keys and notify my landlord. The place will be all yours."

"I'll have a constable get your keys first thing in the morning. When you give me the landlord's name and number, I'll call him myself."

"Great!"

"Are you well enough to come to my office tomorrow afternoon?"

"Absolutely! I'll be there whenever you want, Superintendent."

Felicia was elated. *Wonderful! Maybe I will have an inside scoop on solving the murder of Amadeus!*

Superintendent Green requested all available closed-circuit

television video footage for the day leading up to the carbon monoxide poisoning and during the emergency response. *Wonder if this miscreant hung around to watch his handy work? Would be grand to see him on the CCTV footage!*

The next phone call Superintendent Green made was to his counterpart, Superintendent Jones in Portree. "Hello, Marcus, I've an update on the Amadeus case. Someone tampered with Felicia Friday's gas wall heater while she was out, but she's okay. Lucky for her, the landlord had installed a CO detector. Her article from Skye seems to have reawakened the killer."

"Dear God!" Jones groaned. "I'll put safety surveillance on Amadeus' family and the American tourists."

"Just what I was going to recommend. I'll research this article again, plus our case notes for clues to what triggered the killer to strike again."

"I'll do the same here in Skye and talk to you daily for updates."

Jones leaned back in his desk chair to review the article by Friday and wonder why the killer was compelled to strike again. *Luckily, the intended victim survived. I'll need to put guards on the B&B where the Americans are staying, as well as the entire Mac-Cann family. Wonder if I need to guard my brother, Mattias? Never hurts to be extra cautious.*

His first call was to Phyllida Walker. "Hello, Phyllida, bad news. The poison pen article by Felicia Friday has caused our Amadeus killer to strike out at Ms. Friday."

"Oh, heavens! Is she okay?"

"Yes, luckily there was a carbon monoxide detector in her building. Do your rooms in the B&B have gas wall heaters?"

"No, they have radiators that are turned on in the evening and off all day. Prudence, Vanessa, and Yuri are in the room, by the way. Can I put you on speaker?"

"Yes, please. Hello, everyone, I'm assigning round the clock protection for all of you. Felicia Friday is recovering from carbon monoxide poisoning. Someone tampered with her gas heater while she was out on an assignment."

"Oh my God!" Prudence exclaimed.

"This nightmare just keeps getting worse!" Vanessa rested her head on Yuri's shoulder.

"A guard will examine each of your rooms, and another guard will be stationed in the hall to prevent anyone from entering without your permission. Please check in with the guard if you plan trips. I recommend remaining on Skye for the time being."

"Thank you very much, Superintendent," Phyllida responded. "We're very grateful. I think the killer was initially motivated by past resentments of Amadeus' callous treatment of people who loved him. The Friday article may have stirred up further resentment on behalf of these people originally wronged by Amadeus. I believe the killer became enraged by the mean-spirited suspicions cast by the innuendos in the Friday article. Of course, you're the expert at dealing with criminals."

"Thank you for your thoughts, Phyllida. I've got to get on with setting up protection for you at the B & B and for the MacCann family."

"We'll cooperate in every way we can," Prudence emphasized.

Superintendent Jones' next phone call was to William at the MacCann estate to give the alarming news and plan for protection. Luckily, the four children were still on the estate with their mother as she adjusted to being a widow.

Superintendent Jones finally called his twin, Mattias, with the news and plans for his protection.

"Bloody hell, Marcus, that reporter has stirred up an amazing bit of trouble. Her innuendos have come back to bite her. She's lucky to be alive!"

After assigning police for those needing protection, he studied information involving gas heaters. *How much does someone have to know to accurately manipulate a gas heater into emitting carbon monoxide? Seems Health and Safety recommends having a plumber install a heater to ensure safety. Yet, it only takes a half inch movement to block the air intake valve if you know what you're doing.*

Meanwhile, back in London, Felicia Friday was preparing to meet with Superintendent Green of Scotland Yard. *This is so exciting! I've never been to Scotland Yard. I'll have to be uber observant to write my follow-up article to my own CO poisoning. Maybe this will get me out of hot water with Ogilvy.*

Felicia rode to the meeting with Superintendent Green in an unmarked police car. She was wearing her red suit with white trainers this time. Constable Smith guided Felicia through the restricted doors and up an elevator to the third floor into a tidy office where she introduced her. "Ms. Friday, this is Superintendent Green. Shall I remain, Sir?"

"Yes, Constable, please take notes."

For the second time, Felicia felt small sitting across a large desk as Superintendent Green returned to his chair after shaking hands.

"Now, Ms. Friday, tell me when you first became interested in reporting about Amadeus."

Superintendent Green settled in his chair with hands folded and an encouraging smile. His blond hair was turning grey at the temples. His light blue eyes looked kind on a handsome, weathered face.

Felicia spoke quickly, "You realize, Sir, that I am a reporter. I sometimes initiate my own assignments. I heard Amadeus was planning a grand tour with nostalgic music from the sixties and seventies. He had quite the reputation as a ladies' man with a habit of leaving brokenhearted women behind. I decided to dig a little deeper and found snarky comments about Amadeus' illegitimate child posted on his Facebook page. When I checked further, I found a reference to an American ballerina. It seemed newsworthy. I managed to stumble onto the American mother of the ballerina vacationing in the UK. I simply reported the news as I saw it."

"May I call you Felicia?"

"Of course, Sir." Felicia felt herself relax in her chair.

"Well, Felicia, you are aware that each place you observed the American ex-lover and her friend, you were there as well. This could appear as suspicious behavior or worse, stalking."

"What! No! I simply observed and wrote what I saw." Felicia stuttered and felt sick.

"Everywhere you accuse the women of being, you were there as well. Were you possibly creating some of your own news for a more salacious article with a desire for a scoop? Did you possibly study the Palladium before the Amadeus concert with a desire to just injure and not kill?"

"Good God, no!" Felicia was now in tears. "Do I need a solicitor, Sir?"

"That's a good question. Do you?"

"Oh, Sir, I'm just trying to be a good investigative reporter. I wouldn't kill someone for a story."

"I really hope not; however, you were also at the location where you imply Prudence Silver and Phyllida Walker had an opportunity to murder Amadeus. You also had the opportunity to commit murder. In fact, as a London reporter, you probably know the Palladium and the dressing room locations, don't you? Did you possibly put on a stagehand jacket and step into the dressing room, close the window and shut the door with a heater emitting carbon monoxide?" Superintendent Green was leaning across his desk with his fist outstretched.

"Oh God, no, I wouldn't kill anybody for a story."

"Make them a little sick, maybe?"

"No! Of course not! You've got to believe me!"

"How much do you know about gas heaters?"

"Absolutely nothing. Please, Sir, why are you doing this to me?"

"Pretty unpleasant, isn't it? Yet you have accused two older women from America with the same circumstantial evidence. Your articles have obstructed a police murder investigation and created God knows how much expense. I don't believe you killed Amadeus, but your articles have been misdirecting Scotland Yard in our attempts to find who did murder Amadeus."

"Sorry, Sir. I was just expressing 'what if' ideas."

"As of this moment, you are to stop interfering with our investigation of Amadeus' murder or I will truly charge you with wasting police time and I promise it will be made public. Do you think your boss would appreciate that?"

"No." Felicia was now sobbing with tears streaming down her face.

Constable Smith took pity and produced a box of tissues.

"Constable, you may drive Ms. Friday back. Felicia Friday, no more stalking. Not another word in print or otherwise regarding Amadeus' murder. For the time being, no writing about your own near miss with carbon monoxide. I need to turn all my attention to doing some real detective work. Understood?"

"Yes, Sir." Felicia got up with a wad of tissues, trying to stem her flow of tears.

Back to Basics: Who Killed Amadeus?

Superintendent Green waited for the elevator to close before calling his colleague, Superintendent Jones. "Marcus, we've got to look at the Amadeus case with fresh eyes."

"Right you are. I feel like we're missing something crucial. We've been sidetracked by Ms. Friday's outrageous accusations. With Phyllida Walker and Prudence Silver eliminated as suspects, the evidence looks very different. Along with this, Ms. Walker mentioned something we should check on."

"What's that?"

"She suggested the murderer attacked Felicia Friday because they were offended by her harsh remarks about Prudence Silver and Amadeus' daughter, Vanessa Silver. They felt protective, if you will, of the victims of Amadeus' overzealous love life."

"Not sure if that's so, but I'll give it a think."

"I'm going to visit Amadeus' valet again to review Amadeus' early years and his love interests. I hope to avoid having the same discussion with Amadeus' wife, Florence."

"It's worth a try. Give me the list of former lovers. Two heads are better than one."

"Of course. I'll tap into the Skye rumor mill."

"Cheerio and out. I have a meeting with Scotland Yard's higher-ups. The problem with Felicia Friday's innuendos is that some people believed her. Hopefully, she will direct her attention elsewhere. I gave her a serious warning."

"Pity I wasn't there to see it for myself. Really hope she heeds the warning."

Superintendent Jones phoned William. "William, my man, we're still trying to discover who killed Amadeus and I need your help. I need detailed information about Amadeus' love life. How far back do you go? Did you know him when he was simply Fergus MacCann?"

"I knew Amadeus when he was Fergus. He and I were in sixth form at school together, but not close friends. I hung around, played bass, and sang backup with his group when I could. As he became famous, I was the one who kept track of business and performance dates. I'm organized and love working behind the scenes. Amadeus compensated me handsomely to keep order in his chaotic musical life as well as his considerable business success. You think the murder goes this far back?"

"Just a thought. Could you possibly know about love interests that far back?"

"He was always a 'Jack the Lad' who would sleep with the most available girl."

"Blimey! Do you have some names?"

"It might be better if I come into the station. I don't want to be overheard at the estate."

"Just what I was about to suggest. Are you available tomorrow? Would Florence know of any other girlfriends who became pregnant or had a child?"

"Lord no! Amadeus was very careful to shield her from his escapades, as he called them. Please try not to upset her. She's been brave and gracious with Vanessa Silver, but I'm not sure she could manage any more illegitimate children."

"I can't promise anything, but for now I'll depend on your man-to-man relationship with Amadeus."

"I'll be there at 10."

That'll be grand, William."

Superintendent Jones closed his door and leaned back in his chair for a serious think. *I wonder if William resented being pushed behind the scenes as Amadeus became so famous. I suspect Amadeus could be a difficult person to work for. I was just young enough not to be paying attention to Amadeus. However, the music was great. Maybe I'll brush up on Amadeus' past by watching Felicia Friday's television programs. A detective's job can be obnoxious sometimes. Just because misery loves company, I'm forwarding these telly videos to my buddy, George Green.*

Back in Scotland Yard, George Green returned to his office just in time to discover videos from his counterpart in Skye. *Bloody hell! I can't face Felicia Friday twice in one day. Time for me to head home.*

Before he left the office, Green sent Jones the CCTV coverage near Felicia Friday's flat. He didn't recognize anyone. Piccadilly Circus was always crowded and bustling.

Felicia Friday returned to her hotel to recover from her ordeal with Superintendent Green. *That man is such a bully. Now, I'll have to drum up some reason not to write about the Amadeus case. I've spent time and money for nothing! Damn! I'll call the boss right now.*

"Hello, Guv, thanks so much for covering my stay here. Scotland Yard wants me to hold off on any story about my jimmied heater while they follow some leads."

"Brilliant, Felicia. I have some London follow-up to the excellent piece you did on the orchid donations at Kew Gardens."

Felicia sighed as she closed her phone.

Gossip on Skye

On this cloudy, overcast day, Phyllida and Prudence decided to visit a pub known for its oyster stew. Vanessa and Yuri were reviewing a video of a complex choreography from the Scottish Country Dancers as they prepared for another Saturday dance.

The pub smelled wonderful with the aroma of the seafood, Skye Gold ale, and a peat fire. The ladies were seated near the fireplace, which felt especially cozy on this dreary day. They were near a long table with a group of people having a special lunch for a woman retiring from a local whiskey distillery. The retiree of honor received a lovely gold watch. She expressed her great love for her co-workers.

"You really are a dear part of my life, my family that I truly love."

As the group departed with great cheer, a woman at another table spoke loudly to her hard-of-hearing partner. "That's Sheila Mackenzie, you know. Her daughter, Camilla Mackenzie, is a radio presenter. She sang with Amadeus in the early days. Rumor has it Camilla became pregnant by Amadeus, but the termination went wrong. I heard that Camilla turned down a marriage proposal because she couldn't give the man a child."

"I heard the same thing. I wonder if Camilla's bitter. I would be."

Both women stopped talking as their lunch arrived.

Prudence and Phyllida looked at each other. Prudence broke the silence. "Wonder how bitter that would make a woman? Would she know how to manipulate a heater to cause carbon monoxide poisoning?"

"I'm just going to jot down this information while it's fresh in my head." Phyllida pulled a small note pad and pen from her purse. "Could she be the mysterious Facebook messenger?"

"Damn Amadeus! I wonder how many lives he altered with his overactive libido!" Prudence buttered a roll angrily.

Happily, the oyster stew was as good as rumored. After a rhu-
barb cobbler with Earl Grey tea, the women were ready to take a
long walk back to the B&B.

"I think I'll look up Sheila and Camilla Mackenzie before calling Superintendent Jones. Have you and Vanessa been checking
your Facebook pages for strange comments?"

"I'll get right on it, Philly."

Back at the B&B, Phyllida looked for both Sheila and Camilla
Mackenzie. "Pru, do you recognize this lady, Camilla Mackenzie?
I seem to remember her from the funeral."

"Let me look. Yes, she sang at the funeral. I'll check with Vanessa to see if she spoke with Camilla."

After a light dinner in their room, Vanessa and Yuri joined
Phyllida and Prudence to look at the current Facebook entries.

"No, there are no strange remarks in my Facebook entries.
Look, Yuri, your mother has posted pictures of the boys playing
in Lone Mountain Park."

Phyllida opened her laptop and pulled up the pictures of both
Sheila and Camilla Mackenzie. "Anyone recognize these ladies?"

"Heavens, that's the strange woman who wanted a selfie with
me just after Amadeus' funeral. You say she had a termination from
a pregnancy by Amadeus and she couldn't have children after?
How incredibly sad! I wonder if she pretended I was her child."

"That's really messed up, Lubchik. We might need to get protection from her. Who's going to notify Superintendent Jones?"
Yuri looked pointedly at Prudence and Phyllida.

"We are," the women said in unison.

"I'll leave a message for Superintendent Jones right now.
I'm going to see what I can learn about these women. Camilla's
behavior certainly sounds strange." Phyllida reassured all as she
picked up her phone.

Prudence was clasping her hands nervously. "What would we
do without your ingenious snooping, Philly?"

"See you in the morning." Phyllida opened the door to her
room to drink cocoa and watch late night telly.

"When Superintendent Jones phones, I want to speak to him personally about extra protection for Vanessa," Prudence instructed Phyllida.

"Protection for all of us, Mother," Vanessa spoke forcefully.

"Damn! That nut case was around all of us! We were clueless. The police should have been on top of this!" Yuri hugged Vanessa.

Superintendent Jones received Phyllida's message and called her that evening. Phyllida related the discussion she and Prudence overheard about Sheila and Camilla Mackenzie. "Superintendent, we're feeling really nervous about someone like Camilla Mackenzie harboring long-term resentment."

"I see your point, Phyllida. I was already arranging protection. There'll be a constable in the hall outside your rooms within an hour."

"I'll let the others know. We'll all sleep better tonight."

Quiet Trip to Edinburgh

After sending security to the B&B, Superintendent Jones researched Camilla Mackenzie. She was employed as a radio and sometimes television presenter in Edinburgh. He then contacted Sergeant Ann MacLeod to plan early morning travel. "I'm not naming the destination or the person we'll interview. We should return the following day. I don't want to lose the element of surprise."

"Right, Sir. I'll be ready. Should I be in uniform or civilian clothes?"

"Definitely civilian clothes. We'll pick you up at 600 hours."

Then he called Superintendent George Green. "Hello, George, I want you to know I'm traveling to Edinburgh to interview Camilla Mackenzie. Mum's the word." Jones then filled his London counterpart in on what Phyllida and Prudence had overheard.

"I won't spoil the surprise. Just be sure to fill me in on the details afterwards."

Superintendent Green looked up Camilla Mackenzie, then wondered why they hadn't thought of her before. *Ms. Friday's attempt to be sensational really delayed good detective procedures.*

Superintendent Jones and his wife picked up Sergeant MacLeod at 600 hours as promised.

"My wife is driving us to the airport to catch a flight to Edinburgh. We'll be interviewing Camilla Mackenzie at work and at home." Superintendent Jones then repeated the information that Phyllida and Prudence had overheard.

"Heavens, Sir, I've heard the same rumors, myself. Don't know why I didn't think to connect it to a resentment of Amadeus. Possibly because so much time has passed. Wonder what reawakened the resentment – if she murdered Amadeus."

"Good point. What awakened the sleeping tiger?"

They arrived in Edinburgh during rush hour and drove in a

rental car to the Edinburgh Police Offices, housed in a modern structure amid many older grey stone businesses.

Superintendent Jones asked for his counterpart, Superintendent Kathryn Nevis, whom he knew from several Scottish training sessions over the years.

"Hello, Marcus, what a pleasant surprise." Superintendent Nevis was a tall woman, wearing a fashionable grey pantsuit. She crossed the room to shake hands.

"Great to see you as well, Kate. This is my Sergeant, Ann McLeod. We're here to follow up on a lead in the Amadeus murder case."

Sergeant MacLeod shook hands and noted the firm hand of Superintendent Nevis.

"I'm asking a huge favor. I want to interview Camilla Mackenzie at her workplace at the Forth Radio and Television Station, then follow directly to her townhouse nearby. We need a search warrant on short notice. Do you know a judge who will accommodate us? I know I'm asking a tremendous favor." Superintendent Jones placed his hand on his heart as he spoke.

Superintendent Nevis took a deep breath and returned to her seat behind a large desk, while motioning her two visitors to be seated in chairs positioned in front of her desk.

"What compelling information do you have for me to sway the judge?"

Superintendent Jones relayed the overheard gossip and furthered this information with the strange behavior as Camilla Mackenzie approached Vanessa Silver for a selfie just after Amadeus' funeral.

"Certainly odd. I'll try my best with a helpful judge I know." Superintendent Nevis looked up a number and dialed.

"Good morning, Vivien. I'm sitting with Superintendent Jones and Sergeant MacLeod from Skye. They're investigating the murder of Amadeus. They learned some interesting information and want to follow up without much advance notice." Superintendent Nevis relayed the rumors and the strange behavior. "I understand that gossip about an incident from over thirty years ago doesn't seem like an emergency; however, there was that strange behavior at the funeral. Best to be thorough with the investigation. Thank you so much. I'm sending the Skye representatives upstairs to get the warrant right now."

"Kate, you are a jewel, and I'll be in your debt." Superintendent Jones let out a breath he didn't realize he was holding.

"I intend to call in a favor as soon as I can, Marcus. Vivien Chan's office is on the fifth floor. Her clerk will meet you at the security window. Good luck. I often listen to Camilla Mackenzie. I hope you don't find her guilty of anything."

The judge's clerk was standing at the security window as the elevator opened. "Superintendent Jones and Sergeant MacLeod? Come with me, please." The young man was wearing a black suit with white shirt and tie in contrast to his very young looks.

As they entered Judge Chan's office, an Asian woman with her grey hair in a bun and a pearl collar on her navy dress was signing the warrant. "My parents are fans of Camilla Mackenzie. I really hope you find her innocent. Also, no malicious news articles, please. Some paper out of London keeps printing the most bizarre conclusions."

"My colleague in Scotland Yard gave this rogue reporter some very stern advice about the consequences of interfering with police investigations, plus the consequences of libel. There's been serious interference with this investigation because of her misleading stories."

"I really hope that quieted her. Here's your warrant, Superintendent." Judge Chan walked out from behind her desk and handed it to Superintendent Jones. She shook hands with her two visitors before returning to her desk piled with neatly stacked files.

The Forth Radio and Television studios were a short drive from the police station. Without showing police identification, Superintendent Jones asked to see Camilla Mackenzie. He and Sergeant MacLeod signed the visitor's register. A security guard directed them to a room just outside the glassed-in cubicle where

Camilla Mackenzie was sitting with headphones and speaking into a large microphone. Her engineer sat on the opposite side of the desk, watching a monitor.

"You here to visit Camilla?" a man asked.

"Yes, we're hoping to have a word with Ms. Mackenzie when she finishes. I believe her show is over in 10 minutes," Superintendent Jones replied.

"Sure, just sit here. Want me to turn on the sound? My name is Gary. I'm the station manager."

"Yes, please! I'm Marcus Jones and this is Ann MacLeod." They all shook hands as the visitors were seated.

Camilla Mackenzie noted the visitors looking in as she concluded her show. *That man looks familiar, but I can't place where I've seen him. Probably a fan from one of my in-person promotions. Thank God I've had my roots touched up.*

The Skye police saw a very buxom woman with intense red hair, wearing a red V-neck sweater and straight, black leather skirt. She approached with a smile. "Hello, I recognize your faces, but I don't place where we met."

Superintendent Jones stood up and presented his warrant card, as did Sergeant MacLeod.

"As you probably know, the Amadeus murder is still unsolved, so we're gathering further information from people who knew him. You might know something that can help us, Ms. Mackenzie. We understand you sang with him when he was still Fergus MacCann."

"Oh, and here I thought you were fans." Camilla sank into an empty chair, facing the two Skye police. "Yes, I sang with Amadeus in the early days. Many Skye singers and musicians sang the old Elvis faves when they were getting started."

"Of course, we plan to interview many people who worked with Amadeus. We believe you had an experience with Amadeus that might cause some long-term pain and resentment. Would you like to have the rest of this conversation in the privacy of your home? I understand you live nearby."

"Uh, my place is a bit messy. Could I straighten it a bit before you come in?"

"Actually, we have a warrant to examine your home. We can drive you there and have a look; the housekeeping won't present a problem."

"Am I a suspect?" Camilla looked pale and nervous, her mouth trembling.

"We want to eliminate you from our inquiry. We'll be getting information from many acquaintances of Amadeus."

"Okay, I walked to work today. You can drive me home. My building has a reserved parking space for visitors. I hope you're not in a marked vehicle." Camilla put on her leather jacket as she spoke.

"We're in a nondescript rental." Superintendent Jones gestured for Camilla to lead the way to the car park. "The white Prius is ours."

Sergeant MacLeod held the back door for Camilla to enter. All were quiet as Superintendent Jones drove the four blocks. "You must enjoy the convenience of living near work, Ms. Mackenzie."

"Yes, I love being in walking distance." Camilla willed herself to calm down and stop trembling. She clasped her hands and breathed deeply as she often did before a performance. "The visitor's space is close to my front door."

The complex was created from an old Edinburgh church that was converted into condominiums ten years earlier. The grey stone building had individualized entrances with brightly painted wood doors of different colors. Camilla's door was her signature red. She unlocked her door, entered first and quickly sat at a desk with an open laptop computer. She deftly lowered a silver framed photo as she waved the other hand. "The place is all yours, folks. Would anyone care for a cup of tea?"

"No, we're good, Ms. Mackenzie." Superintendent Jones noted her hiding the framed picture and planned to check it later. "Have you had any recent correspondence with Amadeus?"

"Amadeus contacted me about appearing with him at the Palladium, but I had scheduled personal appearances for the station. I sang at his funeral along with Johnny MacKay, though."

"Ah, yes, I remember. It was very nice."

"Thank you. It was a struggle to keep my composure at such a sad occasion."

"I believe you have known Amadeus a very long time. At one time, you and Amadeus were lovers. I've been told you terminated Amadeus' child."

"Yes, I did. I was just seventeen and needed my parents' approval to get a legal termination. I decided to use a woman on Skye to do the deed. An infection set in, and I had to have a hysterectomy. One ill-advised affair and an adolescent's attempt to avoid parental anger completely altered the course of my life. I felt I couldn't marry if I couldn't bear a child. I had always thought of marriage and children as part of my future. Instead, I decided to marry my career. A sad second choice."

"This must cause you an enormous amount of resentment."

"Yes, of course; however, I've been fortunate to have a good life here in Edinburgh. I have a great fan base. I'm part of a circle of single friends that makes a wonderful family."

"Perhaps you'll now show me the framed picture you tried to hide."

Camilla felt tears escape and her mouth trembled as she handed the framed photograph of her with Vanessa Silver. "Seeing her reminds me of the child I might have had. My mother and I both cried when we first saw a picture of Amadeus and Prudence Walker's daughter, Vanessa."

"Your mother cried as well?"

"You see, I'm an only child. My mother would have loved to have a grandchild. As a teenager, I didn't think about my future. I just wanted the problem to go away. Careful what you pray for."

While Superintendent Jones questioned Camilla, Sergeant MacLeod was searching the other rooms – bedroom, bathroom, and spare bedroom – for evidence of an obsession with Vanessa Silver. She found expensive lingerie and clothing, mostly black or red, but she found nothing suggesting an obsession. She silently gestured to her boss with a shrug and a shake of her head.

Before leaving, Superintendent Jones casually asked, "How do you heat your home?"

"Our building shares the old furnace that had heated the church. Surprisingly very efficient. Wait a minute! Do you think I fiddled with a heater to kill Amadeus? I was here in Edinburgh at the time, and I have no mechanical skill. I struggle using a corkscrew to open my wine. That's why I drink more single malt whiskey."

"Sorry, Ms. Mackenzie, we're forced to ask for the record."

"Well, really, Amadeus was a flawed man, but he didn't deserve to die like that. I just hope he didn't suffer."

"Thank you for your cooperation, Ms. Mackenzie."

Unexpected Company

Sheila Mackenzie, Camilla's mother, was still getting used to her retirement. She continued to rise and shower early. Today, she was meeting a friend for lunch. She put on her brown slacks and natural, undyed wool, fisherman's knit sweater. She had just had her hair dyed a soft apricot, close to her former color. Her warm red jacket was draped over a chair, so she was ready for her friend to pick her up. The knock on the door startled her. *It's almost an hour early. What's Millie thinking? Did I get the time wrong?*

She opened the door, ready to greet Millie. "Oh, Angus Gray, I was expecting someone else. How can I help you?"

Sergeant Gray showed his warrant card as he replied, "Hello, Ms. Mackenzie. Constable Smith and I need to ask you a few questions. May we come in?"

"Of course, come in. I'm expecting Millie in an hour. Don't bother showing your warrant cards. I've known you and John since you were bairns. Ask what you wish."

Both young officers wiped their feet on the porch mat and removed their hats as they entered. "We're asking many people about Amadeus, trying to get help to solve his murder."

"I see." Sheila motioned them to be seated. She chose a large, overstuffed chair while Angus Gray and John Smith sat on the settee.

"We've heard that you and your daughter have reason to resent Amadeus."

"Well, all of Skye knows he impregnated my seventeen-year-old daughter. An illegal abortion nearly killed her. If I were going to kill Amadeus, I would've done it back then."

"We understand you and Camilla cried over the beautiful Vanessa Silver."

"Yes, we did. Camilla dreamed that her child might've been beautiful and talented. I didn't have the heart to remind her that she could have had a troublemaking loudmouth like young Fergus MacCann."

"Do you have a picture of Camilla with Vanessa?"

"Camilla gave me a photograph that I keep in a dresser drawer. I'll take it out when she visits."

"Could you show us?"

Sheila heaved a sigh and stepped into her bedroom. They could hear a drawer open, and she returned with a silver framed photograph of Camilla and Vanessa Silver.

"This must be hard for you, Ms. Mackenzie."

"Time has softened the disappointment. Camilla has moved on with her professional life. I'm very proud of her."

"Of course. Thank you, Ms. Mackenzie. We'll be in touch if we need more information."

"Next time, let me know when you're coming, and we can have tea. I make marvelous strawberry scones."

"Sounds tempting."

Both men walked silently to their car. "I don't think Sheila Mackenzie is obsessing over Vanessa Silver."

"No, but I wish she hadn't mentioned the strawberry scones. I'm ready for lunch."

"Remember, Jones ordered us not to discuss our findings with anyone but him. He's probably interviewing Camilla Mackenzie in Edinburgh right now."

Sheila watched the policemen get into their vehicle, then immediately called Camilla.

"Darling, the police have been here questioning me about resentment of Amadeus."

"Superintendent Jones just left my place after a thorough search. He asked questions about my relationship with Amadeus and any lingering resentment. If I were going to murder Amadeus, it would have been after I discovered I was pregnant. My love died in an instant. Amadeus told me I was stupid and immature not to use precautions like a grown woman. Remember, he gave me money to get rid of my problem."

"Exactly what I told the lads that came here. Showed their warrant cards, they did. I've known Angus and John since they were in nappies. They looked very official standing on my front steps. I've got to go now. Millie and I are having a pub lunch so she can give me all the gossip from the distillery."

"Enjoy yourself, Mum. When Jones left, I had the feeling that I'm no longer a suspect."

"Of course. It's so unnerving to know that a killer is out there walking around. Rumor has it that someone fiddled with the heater of that reporter from London. Obnoxious lass, but she didn't get hurt, thank God. There's Millie now. Goodbye, darling."

Superintendent Jones and Sergeant MacLeod drove back to the Edinburgh station to verify that Camilla was in Edinburgh at the time of Amadeus' murder.

"I don't believe that Camilla and her mother are involved in Amadeus' death. I think Superintendent Nevis and Judge Chan will be relieved."

"I'm relieved as well, Sir. My family sometimes listens to Camilla on radio and telly."

"Camilla really does have a large fan base."

As they entered Superintendent Kate Nevis' office, she was just ending a briefing from a constable.

"What did you find out, Marcus?" Kate walked around her desk to greet her visitors from Skye.

"You'll be relieved that Camilla Mackenzie is no longer a suspect in Amadeus' murder, but I need to regroup. I'm running out of ideas. Thank you very much for your assistance in getting the search warrant."

"Anytime, Marcus. Remember, I'll be calling in a favor from you. Let me drive you two to the airport."

"That's a kind gesture I'll gladly accept. But first, I need to reassure Vanessa Silver's family. They became unnerved when they learned that Camilla might be obsessed with Vanessa."

"That does sound creepy."

During the thirty-minute drive to the airport, Kate Nevis pointed out Edinburgh landmarks as she drove up and down the hills of the ancient city with its grey stone buildings, looking like scenes from medieval fairytales.

"There's the Balmoral Hotel. J. K. Rowling stays there to write when she wants peace and quiet away from her husband, children, and dogs at her country estate. It's near the Royal Mile where she used to write in a café. On the other side of the Castle Rock is a very old area called Grassmarket. The White Hart Inn claims to be the oldest pub in Edinburgh. I stayed at the Apex Hotel on Grassmarket Road when I first came to Edinburgh."

Jones and MacLeod were feeling drowsy as they settled into the small plane for their return to Skye. It had been a long day. Now, Superintendent Jones finally had time to read the texts from Sergeant Gray and Constable Smith.

"Sheila Mackenzie appears to be free from suspicion. Although she acknowledged her daughter's fantasy of giving birth to a Vanessa look-alike, she saw the possibility of the child being a loud, obnoxious boy like young Fergus MacCann. Fergus has been quite the troublemaker. Maybe I'll just check what he was doing at the time of the murder."

Superintendent Jones phoned Phyllida from the airport and suggested that he meet them all at the B&B for their seafood night. "I want to assure you that the Mackenzie mother and daughter are free from suspicion in the murder of Amadeus. They are not stalking Vanessa or any of you. However, I intend to keep the constable in the hall and provide security as long as you remain on Skye."

"What a relief! I'll tell Prudence, Vanessa, and Yuri right now. We're watching the Skye evening news together. Look forward to seeing you at dinner."

Double Checking

The following day, Superintendent Jones arrived at his office an hour later than usual. The first thing he did was call Superintendent Green in London. "The Mackenzie mother and daughter are free from suspicion. At the time of the murder, Camilla was visiting a local homeless shelter for women and children. She was live on Edinburgh television, supporting a fundraiser. Her mother was in Portree. I've been thinking about taking a second look at young Fergus MacCann. He's got a record of arrests for starting fights while drunk. He's known for being hot-headed."

"Sorry to disappoint you, Marcus, but Fergus has the tightest alibi. He was arrested at the Palladium for being drunk and disorderly and spent the night in a London cell. His mother left Amadeus' dressing room where Amadeus and William were drunk and asleep to bail him out. As it happens, the death was discovered before Fergus got his freedom."

"So often family members are involved in a murder."

"Right you are, Marcus. However, I don't think family was involved in this case."

"Doesn't seem like it. Any ideas on where else to look? This case really has me stumped."

"I'm stumped as well."

Both detectives spent the day reviewing the Amadeus case. After he returned home, Superintendent Jones decided to watch the videos of Felicia Friday's television interviews and the recordings of the street activity following the carbon monoxide scare at her flat. *Let me see how Felicia Friday twisted the gossip about Amadeus. Plus, maybe I'll recognize someone watching the emergency aftermath in Piccadilly Circus.*

He watched the televised interview of Johnny MacKay and Camilla Mackenzie, which was cut short when they stormed off after Ms. Friday's insulting innuendos. The second video was grainy, and he almost dozed off, watching crowds of people shuffling around the emergency response. Suddenly, he recognized someone and realized this person was also present when Amadeus was at the Palladium. *Blimey! He's been right under our noses all the time! I'm calling Green right now. We need to keep him under surveillance while we get proper evidence.*

Superintendent Green was home at tea with his wife. He recognized the caller. "What can I do for you, Marcus? Damnation! I'll watch the videos straight away! Yes, I'm putting him under surveillance within the hour."

The Tour Bus

The suspect lived in London in a flat near Hyde Park. This tourist mecca was full of hotels with many tourist busses parked along the curbs, so a Grand Tour of London bus appeared perfectly natural. It became Command Central and gave the police clear sight of the entry to the suspect's apartment building and the only entrance to the underground garage. The suspect and his boyfriend returned home near midnight. Both were staggering as they supported each other to the front door. The drunken ballet continued as the boyfriend dropped the key twice, then rang a neighbor who buzzed them in. The sergeant on duty had a quiet chuckle as he watched the pair enter. A light went on inside the fourth-floor flat. Surveillance of the darkened flat continued during the night. The suspect emerged at 800 hours and walked briskly to the nearby Starbucks. He noted a pretty woman walking a Doberman Pinscher in the same direction toward the entrance.

"Beautiful dog, Miss. Is he friendly?" The suspect put out a hand gingerly as the Doberman rumbled a low growl. "Ah, I think not."

"So sorry. He's still in training. I'm watching him for my boyfriend. I'm combining his morning walk with my morning latte."

"Great, I won't get dog-bit if I join you, will I?"

"At ease, Milo. Just stay on my right side and Milo will relax."

He held the door for woman and dog to enter. They sat at a side table.

"You look familiar. I just can't place where I've seen you." Holly smiled apologetically.

"I used to sing with Amadeus on Skye. I'm now an announcer for the daytime women's show, *Women Now*."

"How interesting! I'm Holly, by the way."

"I'm Johnny MacKay. Pleased to meet you, Miss. Got to go. I'm running late." He dashed off with latte in hand.

Holly and Milo walked out of Starbucks as she spoke into her phone, "He's on his way to the Marble Arch Tube station."

"Good job, Holly. Lucky Milo didn't take a bite."

"Yes, he really doesn't like the guy."

As MacKay continued to the Tube entrance, a man in jeans and a leather jacket turned from browsing through post cards on a street stand to follow the suspect down the escalator into the station. He followed the suspect on his way to work and reported to Sergeant Willoughby on the tour bus every few minutes.

On speakerphone, Superintendent Jones and Superintendent Green reviewed the Palladium backstage video footage, looking for their suspect. The video was poor quality, making it difficult to differentiate individuals who were all wearing grey Palladium Stagehand jackets.

Superintendent Jones called his brother, Mattias, Skye's human compendium of local Portree history. "Mattias, tell me what you know about Johnny MacKay and his family. Please don't tell anyone I'm asking about him."

"Okay, the grandfather came to Portree from Glasgow and opened a hardware store. Grandfather MacKay was also a plumber, who often installed indoor water closets as the age of the outhouse was coming to an end."

"Did the grandfather install or repair heaters or furnaces?"

"Oh yes, the grandfather and all his sons worked on all sorts of heaters."

"Any idea if Johnny MacKay did any work on heaters?"

"Can't be certain. It was common to have sons working for their father. I know Johnny was working on becoming a singing star. Rumor has it he was disowned by his father because of his sexual orientation. That's rumor and not fact, mind you."

"Right, brother, you've been a tremendous help."

Meanwhile in London, Holly and Milo were out walking as Johnny's partner left the flat at 930 hours. Walter Watson was also on his way to Starbucks.

"Lovely dog, Miss. Dobermans can be great guard dogs."

"He feels very protective of me and my boyfriend. Mind if I join you? I hate to take a table for one during the rush."

"Certainly. I'm Walter, by the way."

"I'm Holly. Pleased to meet you. I'm new to the neighborhood."

Walter held the door for Holly and Milo to enter. They chose a small table by the wall. Milo seemed to like Walter better than Johnny, since he tolerated a gentle pat to his head.

"May I ask what you do for a living, Miss? You're lucky to have free time to walk this handsome dog." Walter was slowly drinking his mocha in no hurry to leave.

"Actually, I telecommute for a solicitor. I'm a paralegal. Have laptop will travel."

"How fortunate you are, my dear. I am presently a house husband as I wait for my next acting job. I often do commercials and voice-overs."

"That sounds very interesting. How did you get into such a fascinating profession?"

"My partner used to sing with Amadeus. One introduction led to another."

"Wow, you must have enjoyed meeting some great stars. Did you meet Amadeus?"

"Why, yes. Johnny sang with him on his last performance at the Palladium. I was able to join the dressing room party after the show. Such a tragic outcome. Amadeus had such a strong personality. According to Johnny, he often sucked all the oxygen out of the air."

"Is that right? Did you know Amadeus very long?"

"No, Johnny had the history with Amadeus. Quite the woman-izer from early days in his career. Johnny said that some women he knew were really damaged by his overactive love life."

"Oh, I'm sorry to hear that. Amadeus was such a handsome man and great singer. I think my mother had a crush on him, as many women did at the height of his popularity."

"One of his illegitimate children is a prima ballerina with the San Francisco Ballet. Gorgeous dancer with platinum blonde hair.

Amadeus was notorious for his many affairs. No telling how many terminations. Johnny told of a woman whose life was entirely altered after a botched termination of Amadeus' offspring."

"Heavens! That's awful!"

"Yes, it is. Johnny feels Amadeus got what he deserved in the end." Walter made the sign of the cross.

"You don't think anyone deserves to be murdered, do you?" Milo's ears stood up as Holly spoke.

"Oh, of course not. Listen to me nattering on. I need to get back home and check Facebook for any job offers. Lovely visiting with you, Holly."

"My pleasure. Hope we see each other again while I'm house sitting and dog minding."

"That would be grand."

Walter walked briskly away. In Command Central, Sergeant Willoughby watched Walter walk directly to his flat. Holly slowly walked Milo to Hyde Park's dog enclosure where he could get some exercise playing with other dogs. She joined two other police canine handlers as they watched their dogs romp.

"Holly, great job in your conversation with Walter. Superintendent Green is listening to your recorded conversation now. I'll keep you posted when you need to be walking Milo again to meet our suspect or his partner." Sergeant Willoughby spoke into Holly's cell phone ear bud from Command "Tour Bus."

"Right, Sir, I could use a break for lunch and a visit to the loo. Those Starbucks coffees, you know."

"Certainly, I'll have Ralph, acting as your boyfriend on this stakeout, relieve you until 1700 hours."

Holly turned to Ralph, sitting beside her on the bench, "Milo's yours until 1700 hours. You're my boyfriend, by the way."

"Yes, I was listening in to your conversation with the Sergeant." The handsome man, wearing a tweed newsboy cap, took the leash and remained sitting as Holly left for her break.

Green called Jones just after being briefed by Sergeant Willoughby. "Marcus, we heard an interesting conversation with

MacKay's partner, Walter Watson. Watson has a clean record, by the way. Seems MacKay is enraged by Amadeus' treatment of former lovers he impregnated. He's especially upset about the woman he sang with back in the day. Evidently, his friend was left barren after a botched termination."

"That certainly rings a bell. I'm pretty sure that's Camilla Mackenzie. Wonder if there are other women in the same situation?" Superintendent Jones leaned back in his chair as he spoke.

"This is really going to take some serious digging. I'll repeat questioning the Palladium stagehands and Amadeus' dressing room partiers. Stagehands are a tight-knit lot, strong union. The only infraction they'd report is if someone missed cues during a performance."

"Were there any cues missed or other problems that they reported, George?"

"Not that my investigating officers have heard."

"We really need some kind of evidence other than someone being enraged."

"I'll send a new crew of officers to question the stagehands and party attendees. Maybe fresh eyes and ears will come up with something."

Palladium Backstage

The Palladium was dark and closed to the public as it prepared for a new show. This was good luck for the London officers assigned to interview the stagehands. The Amadeus dressing room partiers were interviewed again at the London headquarters of Scotland Yard. Two officers interviewed all twenty stagehands in a backstage conference room, while the stagehands used the interviews as a good excuse for their coffee break. Sergeant Wadsworth decided to win favors by bringing a delicious assortment of croissants.

"How many of you were present during the backstage party after Amadeus' performance?" Sergeant Wadsworth spoke in a relaxed, friendly manner. Constable Bloxham was taking notes. The twenty stagehands raised their hands.

"Were there any stagehands working that night who aren't present today?"

"Old Aldous has retired." A large grey-haired man volunteered.

"Could you give me your name, Sir?"

"I'm Bernard Pincus."

"Do you know where we can reach Aldous today, Mr. Pincus?"

"Sure, we share rooms in the old Roxbury Apartments. We're both widowed, you see, so we decided to share expenses. Want me to phone him?"

"No, thank you. Just give the Constable his address and phone number."

Sergeant Wadsworth continued, "Have there been any changes since the carbon monoxide death of Amadeus?"

"Yes indeed!" exclaimed several men at once.

Sergeant Wadsworth chose a man nearby to question. "Can you tell me what the changes are, Sir?"

Alan Turner, a middle-aged man from Jamaica, volunteered, "We now have several carbon monoxide detectors placed around the Palladium, as recommended by Health and Safety. The gas wall heaters have been removed from the dressing rooms and the heat is all electric. Health and Safety inspects the Palladium at least once a month and takes air samples. We've never been so well protected." A few of the men expressed agreement.

"Glad to hear it." The sergeant took a sip of his coffee. "Are there any additional memories from the night of Amadeus' performance and party that we should hear?"

"We each have to keep our Palladium jackets in secured lockers since Bernie Pincus misplaced his jacket." The group laughed at this until they noted that both officers were looking up with very intense interest.

"Mr. Pincus, can you tell us when you last saw your jacket?"

"I took off me jacket around 2400 hours as I went off duty. Put it in me locker before going home. Next day, I couldn't find it anywhere. Had to buy a new one. Really resented having to buy a new jacket when the old one was perfectly fine."

"Has anybody else lost or misplaced their jacket?"

The room rumbled "No's" as everyone shook their heads.

"How can you distinguish who each jacket belongs to?"

"We write our name on the inside collar of our jacket. My jacket was extra-large. Some of the jackets are smaller. You get used to your own jacket, you know."

"You have provided very valuable information, which we appreciate. Please move to the far side of the room and enjoy the pastries. Constable Bloxham and I will interview each of you separately. We'll start with you, Mr. Pincus."

With a text from Constable Bloxham, an immediate assignment was initiated to interview Aldous at his residence. Aldous had retired due to age and an arthritic back. He provided no new information. He had kept his stagehand jacket, which he showed the constable.

Each of the 20 stagehands interviewed was able to show their jacket. Most were wearing their jackets and could show their name on the inside collar. As the information reached Superintendents

Green and Jones, they became intrigued by the missing jacket.

"Marcus, didn't William remember some stagehand coming in to close the window while wishing them goodnight?"

"Yes, William remembered that. I certainly would like to locate Mr. Pincus' jacket."

"You and me both."

Granny's Closet

The Scots are known for their thrifty ways, and the inhabitants of Portree were no exception. Granny's Closet was on Skye. One man's trash was another man's treasure. The owners, Rufus and Betsy MacMillan, received clothing donations for sale and also donations intended for Oxfam, a British charity that was 100% tax deductible.

Rufus had no scruples as he searched through each Oxfam bag with the saying, "Charity begins at home." He was known to retrieve items he hoped would sell in the store. Oxfam bags often accumulated in the back room until Rufus had time to give them a search.

Phyllida and Prudence visited this store regularly on their daily walks around Portree. In fact, they found some wonderful items in the smaller women's sizes that fit them perfectly. They had each acquired a beautiful handknit fisherman's sweater for themselves and two more as gifts. Out of curiosity, they often expanded their searches throughout the store. They had seen and even commented on the unusual jacket with "Palladium" on its back.

Superintendent Jones and his wife habitually dined with Phyllida and Prudence at the B&B on the seafood special night. This evening, he dreaded giving the update that they were still not released to return to the States due to the suspicions of higher ranks at Scotland Yard. *These innocent women remain the guests of the UK constabulary because of vicious news articles, and, unfortunately, Headquarters still wants them held.*

"Good evening, ladies. It's lovely to dine with you again. I'll try to update you on some new developments. We have a suspect but no direct evidence to pin on him."

"You ladies look lovely in those fisherman's sweaters. I think I recognize Meg's work. She's famous for her knitting craft." Helen Jones smiled. "These are great investments. The sweaters will last forever."

"Really, I'd love to see any other sweaters Meg knitted. Maybe for my grandchildren." Phyllida smiled as she brushed the popcorn stitching, intertwined with cable knit, on her taupe sweater. "Does she do other colors?"

"She does about one sweater every month and charges 500 pounds, regardless of size, in any color she has in her yarn collection. Like I say, you made a wonderful investment."

"Philly and I bought our sweaters for 80 pounds each at Granny's Closet. We were lucky to get these beauties." Prudence was wearing a navy sweater that enhanced the beauty of her turquoise eyes.

As they relaxed with their individual custard puddings, Superintendent Jones updated them on the London branch discoveries without naming the suspect. "We believe the culprit swiped a Palladium stagehand jacket that he wore as he entered the dressing room where Amadeus and William were passed out drunk, closed the window, and wished them goodnight before closing the door. There's a missing jacket with the name 'Bernard Pincus' written on the inside collar. Finding this jacket would be a great piece of evidence."

"Would this be a size extra-large men's grey jacket?" Prudence asked as she sipped her tea.

Superintend Jones remained motionless, holding a spoon mid-air as he stared. "Where have you seen this jacket?"

"Granny's Closet," Phyllida spoke first. "It's in the back in the men's section jammed onto an overcrowded rack. Not sure of the name written inside the collar, though."

Jones quickly lowered his spoon. "Sorry ladies. I have to make an urgent call." He pulled out his phone as he stepped away from the table. "Get someone to Granny's Closet, now! The Palladium jacket is hanging on a rack in the back among large men's clothes. Yes, Get Rufus or Betsy to open the store tonight. I need to know who brought the jacket into the store."

Conveniently, Rufus and Betsy MacMillan lived above their store and were relaxing as they watched the telly. They ignored knocks. Finally, a constable telephoned Rufus and asked him to open up.

"Can't it wait till morning?" Rufus grumbled as he went to the door in bathrobe and slippers. He reluctantly opened the door to the shop. "Tell Superintendent Jones this is a real pain in the arse!"

Rufus and Betsy came down the outside stairs from their apartment to meet the constable and unlock the door.

"Sorry for the inconvenience, Rufus." The constable had known Rufus and Betsy and their store all his life. "We need to find an article of clothing possibly involved in a crime."

"Blimey!" Rufus and Betsy watched in their robes and slippers.

"Tell me what you want, and I'll find it, son," Betsy offered helpfully.

"Aye, found it!" Constable Smith held up the jacket as he dialed Superintendent Jones "Yes, Sir, the name is Bernard Pincus."

Rufus and Betsy MacMillan reluctantly agreed to close Granny's Closet the following day.

The next morning, Superintendent Jones sat at a cluttered desk in the office of Granny's Closet with a nervous Rufus sitting on a large box across from him.

"Sorry, Superintendent, I'm not great at record keeping. I don't keep a list of people making donations. With Oxfam donations, I give people a blank form to fill out for tax purposes."

"I see several Oxfam bags in the back room. How long before they're sent on?" Superintendent Jones was speaking with a casual tone. He could see Rufus was sweating and very nervous.

Betsy slipped into the room and sat on the box beside Rufus. She gently placed her hand on his knee as she began speaking, "Superintendent, we like to sort the Oxfam bags to eliminate things that need to be thrown away. Don't we, darling?"

Rufus picked up on the hint as he replied, "Yes, we always do that."

"Do you also retrieve items that can be sold in your shop?"

"Sometimes." Rufus' face was turning red as he spoke.

"Can we agree this Palladium jacket came from an Oxfam bag?"

"Yes." Rufus and Betsy spoke together.

"I can assure you I will not report you to Inland Revenue." Superintendent Jones was slowly dragging the truth out of Rufus. "When did you receive this jacket?"

"We received this Oxfam bag just about the time of Amadeus' funeral when all the visitors were on Skye. I thought someone from London might be interested. Frankly, I forgot about it after that. It just hung on the large size men's rack."

Betsy nodded her head in agreement.

"You don't keep a list of Oxfam donors?"

They both shook their heads no.

"Do either of you remember any of the donors at that time?"

"Donors were Skye people. I don't think we had any outsiders dropping anything off."

While Superintendent Jones was interviewing Rufus and Betsy, two constables were examining the store and making photo inventory as they searched for anything else that might be of interest in their investigation of Amadeus' homicide.

A constable looked in the door and signaled he had completed the inventory.

Superintendent Jones sighed as he rose from behind the desk. "I hope you keep better records in future." Rufus and Betsy nodded their heads.

Superintendent Jones followed the constables to the rack of extra-large men's clothes to see for himself that there was no significant identification on any of the remaining garments.

"Dammit Rufus, we may have been visited by Amadeus' murderer. You need to start keeping records just as Superintendent Jones said." Betsy was whispering but her look was thunderous.

"We're not the bloody police. We simply receive people's castoffs and offer them for sale."

"We're in a grey area with Inland Revenue when we sort through the Oxfam bags."

"Charity starts at home, Luv. I'll start keeping a list of who donates clothing and Oxfam bags starting today. Lord, I hate bureaucracy!"

"I've prepared simple forms we can use." Betsy showed Rufus the forms on two clipboards.

Before opening their thrift shop to the public, Betsy and Rufus watched Superintendent Jones and two constables leave the parking lot.

The Palladium Jacket was sent via special courier to London. Superintendents Jones and Green insisted that a constable personally deliver the jacket to Scotland Yard's Forensic Laboratory. Scotland Yard sent a marked car to pick up Constable Alexis Alexander at Paddington Train Station. She handed a briefcase with the Palladium Jacket to the forensic laboratory chief, Matthew Cook, in the reception office of the lab. Then, she had a quick lunch in the Yard's cafeteria before her the return trip to Inverness.

The scientists worried that the outside of the jacket had been handled by too many people to give helpful evidence, but it was thoroughly examined anyway. The analysts' greatest hope was finding something on the inside of the jacket with DNA analysis. Sections of the inside of the collar and the inside of the cuffs were removed for the DNA analysis, and the remainder of the inside was examined for hairs and fingerprints. The DNA would require at least two weeks for results.

Dinner at the Black Swan

Holly and Milo met Johnny MacKay and his partner, Walter, near the Marble Arch Tube stop. They had invited her to a Pub dinner at the Black Swan since it allowed dogs. At 1800 hours, the pub was more crowded than usual due to undercover surveillance by Scotland Yard. A table cleared just as the threesome plus canine entered.

"This is good luck. Let's take this table." Holly sat down on the banquette bench by the wall.

"If you don't mind, Holly, I prefer to sit facing the door," Johnny announced. Walter shrugged apologetically while Holly laughed as she rose and gave Johnny her seat. "Being a poof has not always been safe."

"No problem, Johnny."

Milo lounged beside Holly as she read the menu. The waiter stood patiently as Holly read the entire menu. "I'll have the roast chicken. Please substitute steamed vegetables for the mash."

Walter and Johnny shared a steak and ale pie with mash and gravy. The men each had a pint of ale and Holly ordered a shandy.

"The portions are generous here. There'll be plenty to share with Milo." Walter unfolded his serviette as he spoke. Milo looked up and gave one wag of his tail.

"Aye, Milo might get a bite of steak from me as well." Johnny laughed.

"I hear a Scottish accent, Johnny. Where did you grow up?" Holly gave an inviting smile as she spoke.

"Our Johnny grew up on the lovely Isle of Skye. We just visited for the first time in years. Johnny sang at Amadeus' funeral. I spent time sightseeing. Seems a great many Vikings settled on Skye. A wonderful Nordic influence. There's a Scandinavian festival celebrated annually in the fall." Walter spoke enthusiastically as he took a long drink from his pint.

"How interesting. Johnny, do you still have family on Skye?"

"My grandfather, father, brothers, and more cousins than I can count still live on Skye. I come from a long line of plumbers. My family was responsible for installing most of the indoor water closets on Skye."

"Something to be proud of, Johnny. Was there musical talent in your family as well?"

"Everyone played an instrument and sang at gatherings, but I was the only one to make a career with my music."

"Tell us about yourself, Holly. How did you become a solicitor's assistant?" Walter seemed to be the master of ceremonies at the table.

Holly had been counseled to tell as much truth as possible when talking about herself. This led to fewer complications later. "I grew up working in my father's office in our home in Birmingham. He was a solicitor."

"What drew you to London, my dear?" Walter was still leading the conversation. Johnny was ready for a second pint.

"After university, a couple of girlfriends and I decided to share a London flat and see London as more than tourists. Two married and moved back to Birmingham, but I stayed with my little part-time solicitor's assistant job."

"Lucky for your boyfriend and Milo," Johnny quipped.

"Lucky for me as well. Tell me more about growing up on Skye. I've heard Portree is a great place to visit. Did you do any work in your family's plumbing trade?"

"Johnny is really handy for fixing the plumbing and heating in our flat," Walter enthused.

"Portree is a typical small town where everybody knows your business. I couldn't wait to leave. It was okay to visit with my elderly mum and dad this last time. I think they're pleased that I'm well known in show business. It was good to go through old stuff that had accumulated and throw out things that someone else might use."

"Yes, Johnny and I really tidied the old homestead for his

parents. They continue holding on to things that should go, but Oxfam will make better use of what they relinquished."

The conversation quieted when the food arrived. Holly gave Milo a bite of chicken and Walter gave him several bites of steak during dinner.

After dinner, Holly left her companions to take Milo to Hyde Park's dog park.

"Good work, Holly. You're off until noon tomorrow. Ralph will take Milo." Sergeant Willoughby at his tour bus command post had taped the conversation at the Black Swan and forwarded the recordings to Superintendents Green and Jones.

Superintendent Jones had remained at his desk to receive the latest information from the Black Swan dinner. "This is grand! We can document Johnny MacKay taking bags to the thrift shop for Oxfam. This coordinates with the Palladium jacket donated to Oxfam at Granny's Closet. Wish we could get more specific information about his knowledge of gas heaters before we call him in."

Green was equally pleased. "Would be grand to hear him state, himself, how angry he was with Amadeus."

"We need to be patient. Holly is doing a wonderful job of drawing out the information."

London Confusion

At 1230 hours, Holly was walking Milo past Starbucks when she heard her name.

"Holly, over here, my dear." Walter sat under an umbrella at an outside table. "Do you have time to chat?"

"Always time for you, Walter." Holly smiled as she sat down. "By the way, thank you so much for buying dinner last night. You were very sneaky. I had no idea the bill was paid."

"Our pleasure, Holly. You're such good company. Sorry Johnny was so moody."

"Oh, I hadn't noticed," Holly lied.

"Kind of you to say. He had a call from his parents on Skye that upset him."

"Is that right?" Holly restrained her curiosity to sound casual.

"It seems an item found at the local thrift shop where we dropped off our Oxfam bags was linked to Amadeus' murder by the police."

"Oh, my!"

"Oh my, indeed. Johnny is very nervous that something will cause his family or him to become suspects."

"Really, so sorry to hear this." Holly was digging her nails into her palm under the table to keep from leaning forward as Walter spoke.

"Johnny's a nervous wreck at the best of times. There's nothing I wouldn't do to protect him. He's so dear to me." Walter dabbed tears from his eyes as he spoke.

"Johnny's very fortunate to have your love, Walter." Holly hoped her empathy would allow Walter to share more.

"Let's walk and talk. How about we go to the Hyde Park dog run?"

"If you want to go to the dog run with Milo and me, I'd enjoy that." Holly spoke loud enough to make sure Sergeant Willoughby heard. She prayed the place would not look like a police hangout when she walked in with Walter.

As they slowly walked toward Hyde Park, Walter insisted on taking Holly's plastic bags to tidy up Milo's poop. He was an old-fashioned gentleman.

Sergeant Willoughby hurriedly phoned the back-up police at the Hyde Park dog run. As Holly and Walter walked into the run, they saw a very elderly lady with her toy poodle. Walter tipped his hat to the lady as they sat on an adjacent bench.

"You see, Holly, Johnny is really compulsive when he's had a bit too much to drink." Walter picked up the conversation as he and Holly sat on a bench, watching Milo play with the toy poodle. "It seems he might have absconded with a souvenir from the Palladium. He was very nostalgic about the old singers joining Amadeus at his farewell tour. Johnny's voice sounds as youthful as it was in his twenties. Amadeus' voice lowered from a high to a deeper baritone. My ear isn't that great, but Johnny could tell."

"Is that right?" Holly was searching for comments to help the conversation move along. She knew not to suggest anything that would later be considered "leading the witness."

"Yes, Johnny took a souvenir from the Palladium. When we were in Portree, he thought better of it and put it in one of those Oxfam bags. Somehow, the police have found it and may jump to some alarming conclusions."

"Oh heavens!" Holly hoped that digging her nails into her palm hadn't drawn blood.

"What are thrift shop people doing going through the Oxfam bags anyway?"

"No idea." Holly forced herself to breathe normally.

Holly's walk in the park with Walter provided some interesting facts to further suspicion of Johnny MacKay. Sergeant Willoughby again alerted Superintendents Green and Jones about the conversation.

Superintendent Jones spoke with his counterpart in London. "Might as well wait to see what comes next, George."

"Looks like Johnny and Walter may hang themselves if we give them enough rope."

Forensic Evidence

Superintendents Green and Jones were on a conference call with Scotland Yard Forensic Chief, Bart Bradley. Bradley explained, "The examination of the Palladium jacket is complete. There's DNA evidence that shows two males were in contact with it. One DNA match is Bernard Pincus. The other male DNA is not in our system. If you provide DNA of the suspect, I'll run it. The hairs and fibers are consistent with the backstage of a theater. No surprise there. Nothing showed anything from Amadeus or his manservant, William."

Jones spoke first, "Is it time to call in Johnny MacKay, or do we get his DNA on the sly? I recommend the latter, while Holly continues to stay in touch with Walter, who is an amazingly good source of information."

"You have a point, Marcus. Maybe we can have Holly get used cups from Johnny MacKay and his partner, Walter. She's requested to officially become Milo's handler, by the way."

"No surprise that she's bonded with the dog."

"We're getting closer to an arrest. We must tread softly not to violate anyone's rights as we proceed."

"I plan to visit Johnny MacKay's parents in Portree to ask about the Palladium jacket." It was a sunny day on Skye, a lovely day to set the cat among the pigeons.

Jones drove to MacKay Plumbing to see if Jonathan MacKay Sr. was still working. He browsed a bit to observe daily operations. Jonathan MacKay was smoking a cigar in a back office. Apparently, Health and Safety had not been alerted to this workplace health violation. Superintendent Jones knocked on the open door.

The white-haired MacKay Sr. quickly stubbed the cigar in the ashtray as he shouted, "Come on in, Jones. What can I do for you?"

"Nice things you have here, Jonathan. Makes me want to redo my own bath and kitchen."

"Aye, we could bring you up to date and make your good wife very happy with some new features in the bath and kitchen. We're offering special cleaning and inspection of all gas heaters, too. I think we installed yours four or five years ago."

"Aye, you did. Good memory, Jonathan. I'm here about another matter. A stagehand's jacket from the Palladium was found in one of the Oxfam bags you dropped off at Granny's Closet."

"Me son, Johnny, and his friend, Walter, did a bit of clearing out. Accused us of hoarding, would you believe? You live long enough, you accumulate things."

"Did you see the jacket before it went to Oxfam?"

"No, but I've heard that you police found it and are very interested in how it came to be there. The answer is I don't have a clue. Never saw the thing, meself. Now don't you go bothering my wife. She has a touch of dementia and can get easily upset. Johnny and Walter had her wringing her hands every day as they rummaged through our place."

"No, I won't disturb Mrs. MacKay. Sorry she's not well." Superintendent Jones rose and shook hands with Jonathan before leaving.

On the Trail of DNA

Holly and Milo walked the Hyde Park neighborhood as Milo sniffed his favorite shrubs and tree trunks. Holly was carrying a large satchel, equipped with plastic bag, gloves, and cups with lids to collect DNA evidence. She saw Walter entering Starbucks and quickly caught up with him.

"Hi Walter, you're a hearty soul to be out on this drizzly day."

"If you live in London, you don't let a little damp bother you. Milo looks wonderful in his plaid raincoat. Is it Burberry?"

Holly laughed. "No, imitation couture. He tries to avoid me when he sees me pull out his coat. He has a full doggy wardrobe. This raincoat is my favorite."

"You look very handsome, Milo." Walter patted Milo's damp head.

"Mind if I join you? Why don't you find a seat and I'll get our drinks."

Walter took Milo's leash, and they sat at a table near the front window.

"Hello, Holly, grande skinny latte as usual?" greeted the barista with a green stripe in her hair to match her green apron.

"Yes, and a grande double espresso, please."

Holly watched the expertise of the young man steaming the milk to top her drink.

"Cheers." He handed her the drink with heart-design foam on the latte.

She hoped to collect Walter's used cup and have his DNA right away, but the demons were in the details. Walter quickly drank his espresso, rinsed his cup, and filled it with water for Milo.

Damn! I'll have to remember to give Milo a cup of water first next time.

The rain had stopped as they left Starbucks. Holly and Walter walked together for a block. "I'll leave you here, my dear. This is my laundry day."

"See you later, Walter." Holly walked off her frustration as she and Milo returned to the Hyde Park dog run.

"Here comes the best dressed dog and his pretty handler." Ralph teased Holly. "Glad to see you and Milo are prepared for the London rain. Did you get any DNA evidence?"

"Not yet. I'm bound to get something soon if we continue to visit Starbucks. They know me by name now. Milo and I are regulars. I'll try to be nearby when Johnny MacKay returns. He usually stops for a pint at the Marble Arch Pub before going home."

Sergeant Willoughby was listening in on Holly and Ralph's conversation. He phoned Ralph. "I want you to follow Johnny for a while. Holly and Milo may look too suspicious with their frequent walks in the neighborhood. He usually exits the Marble Arch Tube around 1600 hours. If he gets a drink, quickly grab the empty glass. Do you have supplies in your briefcase?"

"Yes, I'll be ready. Do either Johnny or Walter smoke?"

"No, it's a pity. Tobacco butts are a great source for DNA," Willoughby sighed. The rain returned. "You and Holly can bring Milo to the tour bus to stay out of the rain and wait for a while."

Johnny MacKay was having a bad day at work. His voiceovers for the big soap commercial were scrapped for a female voice, and he depended on this client for a major part of his income.

"Don't take it wrong, Johnny, but we just needed to freshen up this commercial. A woman doing laundry sounds more plausible."

"Men do laundry as well. You're being sexist. As a matter of fact, Walter's doing our laundry as we speak."

"You'll get your turn with a new product, Johnny. This commercial was getting stale."

Helena Reynolds, the station producer, turned on her red stilettos and left.

Johnny had no choice but to return to his office. He tried to sound pleasant as he answered his phone.

"Hey son, Superintendent Jones visited me at work, asking about the Palladium jacket. I told him I knew nothing about it. Never saw it. Just thought you should know that the police are still sniffing around."

"Relax, Dad, I'm sure they understand you had no opportunity to get a jacket from the Palladium. You haven't been to London in twenty years. This is all you need." Johnny spoke with more confidence than he felt. There was a tight knot in the pit of his stomach, so he decided to leave early. He felt the need for a stiff drink. *Damn! My bottle of Skye malt whiskey in my desk is empty.*

Sergeant Willoughby saw Johnny MacKay exit the Marble Arch Tube station, walking quickly. His hunched shoulders and clouded face seethed with anger.

At the Marble Arch Pub, a small group of regulars, two men and a woman, were standing at the bar. They watched as Johnny walked up to the bartender. "A shot of whisky and ale chaser." Johnny then sat on a bar stool opposite the regulars.

Ralph, who entered just after Johnny, ordered a pint and chose a seat at a table near Johnny, who consumed three whiskeys and two pints at lightning speed. As soon as Johnny exited, Ralph quickly and quietly stored the whiskey and ale glasses in his briefcase with a gloved hand while the bartender's back was turned. Johnny staggered as he made his way home past a Boots, where he filled all his prescriptions, and his favorite café, Doolittle's.

The aroma of a tuna and cheese casserole in the oven and freshly ironed shirts greeted Johnny as he entered the flat. "What would I do without you, Walter?"

"You're not getting rid of me, old boy! I'm here to stay."

"Nice to hear a friendly voice. I've had a beastly day. That young bitch, Helena Reynolds, replaced my voice on the soap commercial with a woman to sound more plausible."

"My God! You really have had a bad day. Let me give you a hug." Walter embraced Johnny. "The food's ready. Let's just sit down and eat." Walter took a small green salad out of the refrigerator and moved the casserole from the oven to the table.

"I'll just drink fizzy water tonight. I've probably had too much to drink already."

Walter opened a large bottle of Pellegrino and poured two glasses. The men ate in a comfortable silence.

The following day, Holly met Walter, who was already at a table on the front terrace of Starbucks. "Hi, Walter, can you save a seat for Milo and me?"

"Of course. Give me the leash."

"I brought a dog dish for Milo's water." Holly quickly produced a small dish and filled it with water.

"Milo, your mistress spoils you."

Holly laughed as she went inside for her skinny latte.

When Walter was ready to leave, he threw his cup into a nearby receptacle. A street person rummaged in the bin to retrieve Walter's cup.

A few hours later, the forensic department of Scotland Yard began the process of analyzing DNA evidence, comparing DNA from Walter's cup and Johnny's mug. The lab informed Superintendents Green and Jones they would get results in two weeks. The anxious superintendents made daily phone calls.

"The chief chemist said to tell you that daily phone calls will not speed the process." The forensic receptionist spoke apologetically.

Superintendent Jones met Phyllida and Prudence at the B&B on the seafood special night.

"Helen is visiting old schoolmates for food, drink, and a good chinwag. I suppose that's how you ladies became such good friends."

"Yes, that's exactly how we became such dear friends. This ordeal of being murder suspects would be unbearable if we couldn't rely on each other."

"Hopefully, we're coming to the end of the murder investigation. We're waiting for the DNA results before we can move further."

"Oh, that's wonderful! I've become very fond of Portree and Skye, but it's time to return home." Phyllida clasped her hands as she spoke.

"Vanessa and Yuri plan to return in three days to begin rehearsals with the San Francisco Ballet for their next program and to rescue Yuri's parents, who are still caring for their two boys. It's been hard to be away from their children for so long." Prudence's cheeks became rosy as she spoke.

"Don't you ladies buy any tickets until Scotland Yard gives the word. The wheels of justice can move excruciatingly slowly sometimes."

Conversation slowed as the food arrived. Prudence and Phyllida enjoyed the boiled langoustine with parsnips, new potatoes, and a butter dill sauce. Superintendent Jones devoured a spicy fish stew.

"I will truly miss the wonderful seafood here. San Francisco has great seafood, but Skye has the best langoustine." Phyllida squeezed a lemon over her plate as she spoke.

"We've made some wonderful friends on our daily rounds. Philly, I think we should plan a good-bye tour."

"Don't be hasty, ladies. Rumors can spread so rampantly on Skye. I don't need someone notifying family members we're about to make an arrest. This could put justice back a few weeks if someone were to disappear."

"Oh, God! I hadn't thought of that. We'll just do our regular walks." Prudence held her finger to her lips.

"It's amazing how Prudence and Vanessa's lives have changed since the murder of Amadeus. Prudence's only desire was to make peace with a former lover," Phyllida shared with the table.

"True, the financial bequest will be wonderful for Vanessa and me. Too bad Amadeus never lived to meet our daughter."

Superintendent Jones regretted telling the women there might be a conclusion to the investigation. "Promise me there will be no further discussion of Scotland Yard's work on this murder inquiry. If word gets out of any analysis, we could have suspects disappearing. You ladies must remain guests on Skye until all is resolved."

Both women nodded their heads.

"We won't mention anything that will interfere with your good work, Superintendent." Phyllida placed her hand on her heart as she spoke, and Prudence raised her hand in salute.

Vanessa and Yuri Return to San Francisco

Three days passed with amazing speed. Phyllida and Prudence helped Yuri and Vanessa pack gifts to be mailed home.

"Hopefully, the VAT tax won't bankrupt us," Yuri grumbled as he prepared another form to clear Customs for both the UK and USA.

"We can't show up empty handed, Luv. Your parents have been wonderful to care for the boys. The boys will be so handsome in the plaid jackets and short pants we bought. Helgi Tomasson will love the Scottish dancing clothes and ghillies for the Scottish ballet production in Program 6, and I need some of these beautiful things to remember Scotland – not just the murder of a father I never knew."

Just as Yuri taped a box, Prudence brought in two more fisherman's knit sweaters for Mikhail and Bella. Yuri shrugged and started another box. "Be sure to let Mikhail and Bella know how grateful I am for their care of the boys. I'm glad you're returning home. Be sure to give one of the fisherman's sweaters to your cousin, Beth. She's been house sitting for three homes. We're going to have piles of mail! Thank God Phyllida talked me into online banking, so my bills are paid."

"Yes, Mother, I feel bad leaving you and Auntie Philly behind, but Yuri and I start rehearsals on Tuesday. I know Superintendent Jones will continue to look after you two. No venturing out after dark unless in a taxi."

On the day of departure, Prudence and Phyllida walked Vanessa and Yuri to the van driven by Helen Jones, taking them directly to Glasgow. They both were dressed in black shirts and jeans with black leather jackets. They each shouldered one carry-on bag. Vanessa and Yuri hugged the two women they were leaving behind. They boarded in Glasgow with a stop at Heathrow in London and then to San Francisco. The couple had been up all night packing boxes to be mailed. They slept the entire trip, awakening in San Francisco.

The U. S. Customs agent checked their passports and said, "Welcome back to America." As soon as they exited Customs, Yuri called his father, who left to pick them up in his Lexus SUV. Outside the International Terminal, Yuri and Vanessa waited for their ride, enjoying the sunny day with a slight breeze. Vanessa took a deep breath as she turned to Yuri, "Thank God we're back home. I really miss the boys."

"Me too, Lubchik. Here's Dad. He made really good time."

"No luggage? I'm not surprised. We have twelve notifications of mailed packages from Scotland for you at home. Bella is cooking and the boys are really excited to see you." Mikhail opened the door to stand and hug Yuri and Vanessa.

"I can hardly wait to see them. You have no idea how grateful we are that we could leave our children in such good hands, Papa." Vanessa was close to tears as she spoke.

"*Spasiba bolshoi*, Papa." (Thank you very much, Papa.) Yuri thanked his father in Russian.

Two blond boys ran out of the house as the car pulled into the driveway. "Mama, Papa," Ivan and Dimitry shouted as they ran with outstretched arms. Yuri and Vanessa knelt to give them the first of many hugs. Bella stood smiling as she waited to hug her son and daughter-in-law.

"You're saints to care for the boys, Mama Bella and Papa Mikhail." Vanessa felt tears slip down her cheeks as she hugged Bella and Mikhail. "I've missed Ivan and Dimitry so much."

As they rushed into the living room, Vanessa and Yuri opened their bags to hand their sons two bears in Scottish plaid and two stuffed "Nessie" dragons. The children carried their new stuffed toys all day and into their beds that night.

"Are you hungry?" Bella gestured to the sideboard, piled high with latkes, accompanied by bowls of applesauce and sour cream; chicken livers with crisp toast points; and homemade piroshkis, stuffed with mushrooms and potato, plus bowls of cucumber and potato salads – a beautiful presentation. The adults prepared plates and sat at the table with Ivan in a booster seat and Dimitry in his highchair.

Back in Scotland, Prudence received six new pictures of Ivan and Dimitry holding their new stuffed toys in Scottish plaids. They cheered, knowing that Yuri and Vanessa had arrived safely. "Ivan and Dimitry have grown so much since we left home. I can hardly wait to give them hugs. I hope Dimitry remembers me."

"Of course, he does," Phyllida assured her friend. "Your grand-children are really adorable, Pru."

An Unexpected Visitor

Superintendent Jones was straightening his desk as he tried to reorganize the Amadeus Murder file. The urge to call the Scotland Yard forensic unit haunted him. *DNA takes too bloody long to analyze.* Callum MacQueen walked into his office unexpectedly.

"Hello, Superintendent."

Superintendent Jones gestured to him to take a seat. "How can I help you, Callum?"

"I think I know who kidnapped me and left me to die in that remote cave. I know you've been sidetracked with the Amadeus murder, but I was nearly a murder victim, myself. I still have fears of country roads at night. Not good for a news photographer. My mates heard Fergus MacCann bragging about getting away with my abduction. He also said that it was too bad I didn't have the decency to die."

"You've got my attention, Callum. Let me take some notes." Superintendent Jones began writing on a long yellow pad. "When did your mates hear this?"

"Last night at the Portree Arms dart tournament. Fergus gets to bragging when he drinks."

"I see. Who, exactly, heard Fergus and just what did he say?"

"My cousin, Dave MacQueen. He's a challenging dart champ. When Dave challenged Fergus, he replied, 'I'm going to beat you. I almost put your cousin, Callum, away permanently. Too bad he survived.'"

"Why does Fergus dislike you?"

"He thinks his first-born son might be mine."

"Is it possible?"

"No, Fiona and I had broken up months before she married Fergus." Callum raised his voice angrily, "Fiona and I never had sex. Fergus is crazy jealous for no reason."

"How about I talk with your cousin and get the names of everyone who was at this tournament? Then, I'll investigate."

"'Bout time someone investigated this, because I check constantly to be sure I'm not followed."

"I'll give you protection while we check this out. Have you considered getting a restraining order against Fergus?"

"I don't think keeping Fergus away will help, since he has mates to do his bidding. Remember, I'm a reporter; it's my job is to get in the middle of things."

"I see your point, Callum. Just let the police do the investigating." As Callum left, Superintendent Jones decided to visit the Portree Arms and have a snoop about. Just before leaving, he phoned Dave MacQueen, who verified that he'd heard Fergus MacCann make the remarks about Callum.

Portree Arms

On a chilly, grey day, usual Portree weather, Superintendent Jones visited the pub. He wore a dark sweater over his shirt and tie under a heavy navy jacket. Winners of the dart tournament were listed on the chalk board in pink and green, showing Dave MacQueen as last night's winner and Fergus MacCann as runner-up. *Wonder how Fergus feels about coming in second?*

The barmaid, Shannon MacDuff, smiled as Superintendent Jones took a seat at the bar. "Hello, Jones. You the policeman or the dancer? We have a fish pie special for lunch."

"I'm the police. The fish pie sounds great with a pint. How'd the dart tournament go last night?"

"Me husband was tending the bar last night. I heard Fergus was drunk, and Mike took his car keys. Young Fergus can be disagreeable at the best of times. Just got his keys back an hour ago."

"Came in second with the darts. Seems his throwing arm still worked."

"Aye, he looked more than a bit hung over today. He had my special Bloody Mary with extra horseradish and me own pickled peppers."

"Sounds like a good cure." Superintendent Jones sipped his pint while an old timer added more about the dart tournament to anyone listening.

"Young Fergus could throw darts all right, and he talked a lot of nonsense about trying to kill some reporter who used to date his wife. Fergus is upset the bairn has brown hair like his mum instead of yellow like his pa."

Jones ate his fish pie slowly, but the pub regulars revealed nothing more. Shannon offered her mother's treacle tart pudding, which was delicious. He returned to the station with a full stomach and spent the afternoon reviewing the forensic information from the Callum MacQueen abduction. They'd found ropes and a scarf not traced to any person. Besides, Fergus MacCann was at Amadeus' birthday party. *Wonder if William can provide info on Fergus' mates and the night of Amadeus' birthday party? I'll call and have him meet me at the station.*

William answered on the third ring. "MacCann Residence, William speaking."

"Afternoon, William. I need to pick your brain again, my man. You want to meet me at the station?"

"Righto, Superintendent. I can come by the station this afternoon. Madam is in Inverness for the day. I'm free until 1700 hours."

"See you soon, William."

An hour later, William was at the door to Superintendent Jones' office. "More news about Amadeus' murder?"

"No, another matter. I'm hoping to learn more about Fergus, Jr. Who are his best mates? Something's come up to suggest Fergus was responsible for the abduction of Callum MacQueen. You know anything about that?"

"Not really. Fergus was at Amadeus' birthday party in April. He was upset that the reporter covering it was Callum MacQueen. Rumor has it he resents Callum dating his wife before their engagement. He suggested that Callum fathered the oldest child, Trey, because the child has brown hair like his mother's. As a matter of fact, he recently ordered DNA testing that verified the child was his. Even so, he continues to resent MacQueen for dating Fiona."

"What you tell me agrees with what I heard. At a dart tournament, Fergus suggested he was the one who orchestrated the kidnapping of Callum by having his mates do it for him. Do you know anything about that?"

"Fergus has mates who will do almost anything for him because of his wealth. Fergus drinks too much and seems to always have at least two sidekicks enjoying the party life. Actually, Fiona is becoming very distressed with Fergus' drunken antics."

"Who were the mates at Amadeus' birthday party?"

William sat in thought for a few minutes. "I'm pretty sure Sean Macken was in the picture, along with his two brothers, Shane and Sam."

"Those lads can be wild. We've had them in the cells for drunken debauchery more than once. Kidnapping Callum and doing great bodily harm escalates things. Callum was seriously injured. Thank God those hikers found him."

"I've no personal knowledge of Fergus bragging about kidnapping Callum. He wouldn't admit to it in front of his mother or his grandfather. If you want to interview Fergus, I suggest before lunch while he is reasonably sober." William looked at his watch. "Please excuse me. I need to make sure tea is ready for Madam when she returns from Inverness."

"I thought there was a cook."

"On her day off, I prepare a salad and omelet."

"You're the Jeeves to the household."

William laughed. "You could say that."

Superintendent Jones walked William to the door. He left the office soon after William. His instincts told him this kidnapping would soon be solved.

At 1300 hours the following day, two sergeants were interviewing the three Macken brothers at their parents' home. Fergus MacCann was at the police station, being interviewed by Superintendent Jones.

Sam Macken immediately declared his innocence, "It's me brothers Sean and Shane what does young Fergus' bidding. I've nothing to do with no kidnapping."

Sergeant Gray stopped Sean from hitting Sam with the back of his hand as Sean shouted, "Shut up you fool! We've nothing to say without our lawyers."

Sergeants Gray and Smith smiled, since they had yet to mention the kidnapping. "We'll continue our conversation at the station, lads."

Sitting in Superintendent Jones' office, Fergus watched the Macken brothers being led to an interview room. "This is a bloody trap! I'm calling my brief! We all want briefs!"

Suddenly, the entire station was in an uproar. Fergus was shouting for his brief while screaming that Superintendent Jones set a trap. Two constables, alerted by Fergus' shouting, rushed to the Superintendent's office. Fergus jumped up and swung at the first constable. He ducked as the second constable grabbed Fergus' outstretched arm and flipped him. A handcuffed Fergus was duck-walked to a cell.

In an interview room, the Macken brothers were on the floor pummeling each other. The constables lifted and handcuffed the three men. Then, the Macken brothers were also duck-walked to the cells.

The desk sergeant blurted out, "What the hell was that all about, Guv?"

"I think Fergus' behavior pleads him guilty to ordering the kidnap of Callum. Now, it's simply a matter of time before the Macken brothers compete to see who can get the best deal for pleading first. Forty-eight hours in lock-up should solve the case. Let me call Callum and give him the news. Wonder if Callum gets the £5,000 reward offered by his paper?"

Extended Vacation

Prudence and Phyllida had been away from home long enough to have their short hairstyles losing their crispness. "Wonder how to choose a salon in Portree? My hair looks shaggy," Prudence grumbled to Phyllida on their daily walk.

"I suggest we ask someone who has a hairstyle we like. My hair needs attention as well."

The women chose a cozy tea shop for clotted cream tea and scone before returning to the B&B. The young woman serving them had beautiful curly red hair in a short cut.

"Excuse me, Miss. We love your hair. Where do you have it done?" Phyllida smiled as she spoke.

"My mother has a salon behind our home. She studied under Vidal Sassoon in London but married a Scot, so here she is."

"How lovely! Can we make appointments?"

"Certainly, let me call her now."

They made appointments for the following day.

"You know the difference between a good haircut and a bad one is about two weeks," Phyllida quipped.

The next day, the women arrived 15 minutes before their scheduled time of 1500 hours.

"Hello, ladies, we have a manicure and pedicure special this week," Lillian James greeted Prudence and Phyllida. Lillian's black hair was cut precisely in a straight bob to her shoulders.

"No thank you," Prudence and Phyllida answered in unison. They patiently waited for their scheduled appointments.

Lillian James chose to work on Prudence's hair. "Your hair reminds me of the Vidal Sassoon cuts, which are ideal for straight hair."

Jessica, Lill's assistant, was cutting Phyllida's curly locks. "I love your curly silver hair, Madam."

Just after being shampooed, the women overheard a customer's comment. "Did you hear that Young Fergus MacCann's in jail for plotting the kidnapping of Callum MacQueen?"

Suddenly, Phyllida and Prudence felt the need to extend their visit with manicures and pedicures.

"Yes," another patron of the salon replied. "Seems the Macken brothers were involved too."

"Young Fergus was always causing trouble. He attended a fancy private school. Luckily, his father had money and influence. Still, I heard Florence complain that the headmaster called at least once a week."

"You think he had something to do with his father's death?"

Prudence and Phyllida held their breath.

"No. He was in jail for starting a fight in a London bar. Never saw Amadeus' last performance. Florence had to bail him out. She blames herself for leaving Amadeus and William to sleep in the Palladium dressing room while she was bailing Fergus."

Two hours later, Prudence and Phyllida emerged, very pleased with their hair cuts. Phyllida had bright red toes and clear fingernails. Prudence chose intense violet for her toes and a softer shade of violet for her nails.

"For a few minutes, I thought young Fergus killed his father. That would have been tragic." Phyllida spoke to Prudence quietly in the taxi.

"I will certainly quiz Superintendent Jones tonight when they join us for dinner at the B&B. This kidnapping must have been before we arrived in Skye."

Phyllida and Prudence joined Superintendent Jones and his wife, already seated at a table in the B&B dining room.

Helen Jones greeted the women. "You ladies look wonderful. I hear you visited London Lill's Salon. People come from all over Scotland to have Lilly and Jessica do their hair."

"Thank you. I'm pleased with my cut." Prudence shook her head to make her hair move as she spoke. "I can see why Lilly is so popular."

"Jessica did well with my curly hair. It was getting to resemble a jumble of corkscrew pasta." Phyllida spoke as she broke off and buttered a piece of roll.

"Superintendent, what's this we hear about young Fergus MacCann in jail?" Prudence leaned forward as she quizzed. "For a few minutes at the salon, we thought we were hearing about the murder of Amadeus."

"No, Fergus was a guest of the London constabulary while Amadeus and William were sleeping in the Palladium dressing room. Hopefully, we'll hear from Scotland Yard Forensics soon."

"Much as I've enjoyed Portree, I'm ready to return home. I've been worried my youngest grandson may not remember me," Prudence grumbled. "If you're ever in San Francisco, Philly and I will give you the grand tour."

"That sounds marvelous."

Bureaucratic Interference

Holly faithfully walked Milo to visit Walter and sometimes, Johnny MacKay, while Sergeant Willoughby and his assistants watched from the tour bus. The forensic DNA analysis seemed to be taking forever.

Holly and Milo were due for canine training to upgrade Milo's water rescue skills. The course was scheduled for two days near Brighton Beach, a favorite vacation resort on the south coast. Eager to take the training, Holly asked to meet with Superintendent Green. Later in the afternoon, she sat in Green's office in her casual walking clothes of denim jacket and pants with a blue and white sweater. Milo was lying at her feet on the carpet. His ears stood up each time Superintendent Green spoke.

"Sir, it would be great to get the water training with Milo. Walter and Johnny seem set in their routines. I can give an excuse of a few days' visit with the girlfriends. However, Sir, I'll do whatever you say. I really don't want to compromise this case, although I have become fond of the old poofs."

"Bloody hell, this training comes at a vital point in our surveillance. Though what's two days while we wait for this analysis? I'll have Sergeant Willoughby continue our surveillance. So, Milo, you'll be a water rescue dog."

Milo raised his head and let his tail thump on the floor. Holly leaned forward and gave Milo a pat on the head and a treat from her pocket.

"Thank you so much, Sir. Milo and I will be right on the job as soon as the training is over." Holly tried not to skip as she and Milo headed for the elevator. *I really love Brighton and the beach.* She gave Milo an extra treat in the elevator.

On the routine walk near Starbucks the following day, Holly saw Walter sitting alone at an outside table. "Hello, Walter, can we join you?" She pulled the chair around so she sat beside Walter, facing the sidewalk.

"I missed seeing you at the park earlier. Milo must've had all four legs crossed."

Holly laughed. "That's a good one, Walter. My boyfriend, Ralph, walked Milo in a different direction. I had some work to catch up on. I'm planning to meet some girlfriends for a couple of days in Brighton."

"You young people have a great time. Johnny and I always say the beach is great, but we both end up sunburned and covered in sand. I guess we're just a couple of fussy old queens."

Holly laughed again. "Would you watch Milo while I get a latte? What can I get you?"

"Better not have another espresso. It'll keep me up all night."

When Holly returned, Milo was lapping water from Walter's rinsed cup.

"Milo, Walter's spoiling you." Holly settled into a quiet silence with Walter and Milo as she sipped her latte.

In another part of London, Felicia Friday was being assigned another society follow-up. "Lady Jane is making another generous donation from her late husband's massive estate. She's donating a cottage near Brighton Beach to the British Land Trust. I would like some pictures of the cottage and the nearby area for our Sunday Supplement." New editor, Josh Dinks, was nervously shuffling paper on his desk as he spoke. He fancied Felicia but knew dating her could present a conflict.

Felicia was flattered and amused as she noted the admiring glances from the new editor. *I wonder if I can get off these beastly society assignments. Lady Jane is saving herself a boatload of taxes with this generous bequest. Brighton Beach sounds great, though. Maybe I'll return with a tan.*

The following day, as Felicia parked her red Volvo at the Pelican Inn, a bus arrived with off duty police officers and their canines. She was intrigued and asked a young man why they were at the inn.

"There's nothing dangerous at this inn I need to worry about, is there?"

"Oh, no, Miss. We're giving the dogs training for water rescue."

"Marvelous, I hope to watch. I love dogs," Felicia lied as she gingerly patted a nearby Malinois on the head.

"Best not to touch the canines, Miss. They're on duty. Look, don't touch."

"Right. See you folks later. Just now I need to catch up with Lady Jane and her entourage. They're donating a cottage to the British Land Trust."

Plover Cottage was a stately, stone two-story building, built in 1900. The cottage could sleep ten guests and had an enormous ballroom, which hosted many dances through the years. Lady Jane was more than happy to donate this cottage and let others deal with the leaky roof, wonky electricity, and antique kitchen.

The deep red carpet and carved wood paneling made a wonderful backdrop for photographing Lady Jane. Felicia's photographer showed a flair for displaying Lady Jane and the cottage at their best. Lady Jane looked marvelous in a cream white linen pantsuit as she stood on the curved wood stairs. Photographs of Lady Jane continued in the garden near a child's tree house. In her article, Felicia Friday interspersed the array of photographs of Plover Cottage and Lady Jane with snippets of history.

Natural curiosity made Felicia quiz the police about their canines. In the afternoon, she sat on a veranda with a gin and tonic and her phone camera. An attractive woman with a handsome Doberman Pinscher ran barefoot up and down the beach, throwing floating dummies into the sea for rescue. Felicia submitted an additional article about the police training their dogs near Brighton Beach with her photographs for the Sunday Supplement.

The Sunday News

Superintendent Green was spending a leisurely Sunday morning at home. His wife was reading the society section of the paper while he was checking the current sorry state of local politics.

"Darling, take a look! There's an article about your police canine unit doing water rescue training at Brighton Beach." June Green handed the paper to her husband.

"Hell's bells! Our entire surveillance of a murder suspect has been blown! I've got to get to the office." He pulled out his phone and called Sergeant Willoughby at the stakeout tour bus. "Have you seen Holly and Milo today?"

Willoughby's heart raced as he heard the alarm in the superintendent's voice. "Holly and Milo are sitting at a sidewalk table with Walter, Sir."

"Does Walter have a Sunday paper by any chance?"

"Yes, Sir. It's lying on the table as he and Holly chat."

"Good God! Holly and Milo were photographed in the society page on Brighton Beach while undergoing canine water rescue."

"Good Lord! Should we create a diversion to get Holly and Milo out of there?"

"Yes, think of something low key so we don't spook Walter."

"Have you been watching the *Miss Fisher Murder Mysteries* on the telly?" Holly asked Walter. "They're set in Australia. Makes me want to visit Melbourne."

"We just love the 1929 setting, and the costumes are spectacular. Johnny and I both want to visit Australia." Walter spoke, then sipped his espresso.

The distinctive phone ring interrupted their Sunday morning lattes and espressos. Holly suspected the call was urgent as she picked it up. "Hello, really? My Dad's at our flat for a visit? He never told me they were coming. I'll be right there, Ralph." Holly turned to Walter, "So sorry but I have to leave. My folks have shown up unexpectedly. See you later, Walter." Holly calmly stood up, put Milo on leash and walked away with her half-finished latte.

Just out of sight, she saw Ralph's unmarked police car sitting at the curb. Ralph urged, "Get in. We've been marked. You and Milo are in the Sunday society page of some rag doing police training."

Holly put Milo in the back seat, then sat beside Ralph. She looked at the paper, folded to show her running on the beach with Milo. "Oh no!" Holly quickly read the article and noted the author, Felicia Friday. "All that hard work upended by a picture at Brighton Beach." Holly was truly disappointed. "Are we sure Walter and Johnny have seen the article? Walter seemed perfectly normal to me."

"He won't be after he sees that article," Ralph grumbled.

Walter finished his espresso and pulled the society section of the paper open to read. It took him a minute to realize the beautiful woman and Doberman training on the beach were Holly and Milo. *We've been under surveillance all this time, and I really felt love for Holly and Milo. I truly loved our visits at Starbucks. Wonder what they're waiting for? I need to get to Johnny before he leaves the flat.*

Walter raced home, clutching the Sunday paper to his chest. He caught Johnny just leaving. "Hello, Luv, Holly and Milo made the paper, and it's not good." Walter showed the paper to Johnny. Johnny sat down with his head in his hands. Walter draped his arm over his shoulder.

"Time to put my plan to disappear into action. I'll sign all my property over to you, Walter."

"Wherever you go, I'm going. I'm old, but the time I have left is to be with you. Don't make me have to beg."

"Somehow, I suspected you'd stay with me. We have to be perfectly calm and appear to be on our usual routine."

"I'm an actor, remember?"

"Right. We need to rid the flat of anything that will indicate where we're going."

The men worked quietly as each prepared a backpack and small satchel. They pulled out the prepared boxes to be forwarded to friends and family and placed them on the kitchen table. The shredder ground as they disposed of receipts and travel brochures.

"You really think the cops will forward things?" Johnny asked Walter.

"Eventually. Maybe after they open and examine them." Walter bit his lip to keep from crying.

Johnny activated the timers on the lights to simulate their daily living while Walter drew all the curtains.

The basement opened onto a lower-level alleyway that led to a street not visible from the tour bus stakeout. They scurried down the stairs to the basement. Once on the sidewalk, they walked quietly to the Eurostar for Paris eight blocks away. They felt some tension disappear as the attendants on the train in the Chunnel changed from English to French when they left Britain for France. In Paris, they took a taxi to the Gare de Lyon train station. They boarded a train for Geneva, where they intended to empty their Swiss bank accounts and catch a plane for Argentina.

The methodical Swiss tellers seemed to take forever, and they were on a tight schedule to catch a plane nonstop for Buenos Aires. They were inwardly frantic, while trying to appear calm. Finally, they took a taxi to the airport with little time to spare.

"I think we'll make the plane," Johnny reassured Walter and himself as the taxi sped through town.

Since they had no baggage, their path through security was uneventful. They were the last to board the plane and take their seats, 42A and 42B.

"With a little luck, we'll be learning to tango before they find us gone." Johnny clinked his glass with Walter's as they finally relaxed on the plane.

They've Vanished

Sergeant Willoughby kept a tight watch on the flat and front door. The curtains were drawn. The lights went off for the night and back on the following morning, without the curtains being opened, and with no sight of Johnny MacKay or his partner. Superintendents Green and Jones conferred with each other about the Brighton Beach article. Nobody had seen Johnny MacKay or Walter since Walter returned to the flat yesterday. The forensics finally provided proof that Johnny MacKay had worn the Palladium jacket.

"If they'd announced that sooner, we wouldn't be in this situation," snarled Superintendent Green to his Portree counterpart.

"Now, how do we get hold of these clever old queens?" Superintendent Jones was sick with disappointment. "They slipped right out from under us."

"I'm afraid they may have left yesterday afternoon after seeing the Brighton Beach article. I'm with a unit going to the flat now. I'll fill you in on what we find." Superintendent Green hung up the phone and holstered his pistol.

Superintendent Jones wanted to visit the MacKay home to see if they could provide any clue as to where their son, Johnny, might disappear, but he would wait for information from London first. Back in London, Superintendent Green and Sergeant Jennifer Wyatt rang the bell to the suspect's flat with no answer. They then rang the building manager, who lived on the premises.

"What can I do for you, Gov'ner and Miss?" The short heavyset man answered the door, wearing a white t-shirt and baggy brown pants with suspenders. "You look official."

"We are official. I'm Superintendent Green and this is Sergeant Wyatt. We're looking for Johnny MacKay. Have you seen him today?"

"Johnny pretty much keeps to himself. Walter's good for a

chat, though. We can check the flat to see if they're in. You'll need a warrant if you want me to let you in the flat, though."

Sergeant Wyatt removed the warrant from her satchel to show to Elias Brown, the manager.

"Oh well, let's go up then." Brown led the way up the stairs to the flat and used a master key to open the door.

Superintendent Green stepped into an immaculate flat. A gray settee was placed against the wall with fluffed pillows, and the coffee table had a glass top over a lace cover. As they walked into the kitchen, they saw a stack of boxes and envelopes on the table, all addressed.

"Looks like they were expecting us. Doesn't it, Sergeant?"

"Yes, Sir, they were terribly neat about it too."

They looked in the cupboard under the sink and found piles of shredded papers mixed with wet coffee grounds.

"Bastards! We're going to have a hell of a time going through those shredded documents. How the hell did they get out without us seeing them? Mr. Brown, is there a back door to this building?"

"Yes, the basement has stairs to an old alley, but nobody uses it."

"I'm pretty sure somebody used it recently. Sergeant, get forensics over to check this door. I'm going to walk up the street and get an idea of where they might have gone. Have someone check for taxi pick-ups along this street and check the CCTV surveillance cameras."

"Sir." Sergeant Wyatt was dialing her cell phone as she walked behind her boss.

"Also have checks at all train stations and airports."

Sergeant Wyatt repeated Superintendent Green's requests to Scotland Yard's forensics unit chief as Green was speaking.

The phone call to update Superintendent Jones left him deflated and angry. He decided not to visit the MacKay family just yet, since he didn't want them to alert Johnny and Walter.

Luckily, forensics review of the surveillance on CCTV showed the two men walking quickly and entering the Eurostar station. It was soon verified that they traveled by the Chunnel train to

Paris. The French police were not so speedy in their check of an entry from London. It took six hours to verify the men's arrival in Paris. Eventually, French Police also let Interpol know the two men boarded a train to Geneva. The Swiss police traced the men's journey to a bank and then to the airport for a direct flight to Buenos Aires.

"Hells bells! These men have a three-day head start and are probably in Argentina with no extradition agreement to the UK." Superintendents Green and Jones were on the phone again.

"Let me visit the MacKay family and determine if they've had contact with Johnny and Walter. Can we see if there are any incoming phone calls from Argentina? I can probably detect something by talking with the elder Jonathan MacKay. On another subject, we should probably free the American ladies to return home with our apologies."

"Lord, I forgot all about these two women who were dragged into this investigation by that damn reporter. In fact, she wrote the article with the photos of Brighton Beach."

"Felicia Friday again! I'll fill you in after I talk with the MacKay family."

"Right. I'll make sure Interpol lists both men as wanted for murder."

After the phone call, Jones prepared to visit the MacKay business, accompanied by Sergeant MacLeod.

The senior MacKay was in his office of the plumbing supply store, as usual. Jones noticed that he looked older with tired droopy eyes and a greyish pallor to his face.

"Superintendent Jones, come in and have a seat. Sergeant, pull over a chair. Is this business or social?" Jonathan MacKay extinguished his cigar as he spoke from his seat behind the big, cluttered desk. "Forgive me for not standing; my back is giving me grief these days. Me wife had a fall and I strained something when I lifted her."

"Sorry to hear that, Jonathan. I'm here about your son, Johnny and his partner, Walter. Have you heard from them in the last three days?"

"I received some money from Johnny from London for his mother's care about three days ago. No message except 'Take good care of Mum. Your loving son, Johnny.'"

"So, you haven't heard from him since he and Walter left London?"

"Where did they go? Vacation or something?"

"I have a feeling it's more than a vacation. Our records show they're in Buenos Aires."

"Wow, Buenos Aires! Sounds like they moved away from UK jurisdiction. Good for them." Jonathan MacKay looked up and smiled. "Thanks for letting me know, Marcus."

"You're obliged to let us know if you hear from them."

"We both know that won't happen. I love my son and wish him well. Now, is there anything else, Marcus? I'm a busy man."

Superintendent Jones and Sergeant MacLeod stood and left as Jonathan MacKay started reading from a stack of papers.

Flying South over the Falklands

As Johnny and Walter dozed 13 hours into a 16-hour flight, a woman in business class rang for the attendant. "Help! Someone – anyone! My husband has stopped breathing." The man was lying limply in his reclined seat. "I don't know what to do! Help! I need a doctor."

The attendant, Jose, announced, "We have an emergency in business class. Any doctor, nurse, or medic please come."

A Swiss doctor led the way with an Argentine physician right behind him. The men checked for a pulse. "No pulse. Help me put him on the floor. I'll begin CPR while you count," the Swiss doctor told his Argentine counterpart.

"Right. I've cleared the airway. You can start."

Jose notified the captain of the emergency while both physicians took turns with CPR.

After 15 minutes with no success, the physicians closed the man's eyes and covered him with an airline sheet. Jose and several nearby passengers made the sign of the cross.

The captain announced, "Ladies and gentlemen, we have a medical emergency. We'll be landing at Port Stanley Airport in the Falklands in a few minutes. Seat backs up and put your tray tables away."

Johnny and Walter looked at each other wide-eyed with fear as they prepared to land in British territory. "If they land and just take off, we could still be safe. Just sit tight, Walter." The men were holding hands as the plane descended and made a bumpy landing.

The stunned passengers sat quietly as uniformed paramedics entered the plane and removed the man on a stretcher. A uniformed constable requested that the attending physicians and the man's wife accompany him.

Thirty minutes later, the captain announced, "Ladies and gentlemen, we do not have permission to take off for three hours.

You are welcome to disembark and remain in the airport lounge. We will notify you when to return to the plane."

Johnny and Walter remained in their seats as people filled the aisle, ready to stretch their legs in the airport. Finally, they were the only passengers in their section.

"Do you gentlemen need special assistance to exit?" Ingrid, their attendant, asked.

"Oh, no, we're just going to continue sleeping, thank you."

"You look familiar, have we met?"

"No, I just have a common face. People say that all the time," Johnny replied, trying to hide his irritation.

"Can I bring you something from the airport?"

"No, thank you." Walter and Johnny spoke in unison.

Both men opened books and began reading as they watched Ingrid exit.

"This medical emergency has dumped us right on British territory. Just pray local authorities haven't been notified of our sudden departure," Johnny hissed to Walter.

"We're both professional performers, so just pretend we're tired old men catching up on our rest," Walter whispered. In fact, the men did fall asleep.

Ingrid joined her fellow Swissair workers in the employees' lounge and office. The fax machine began running, and some of the papers fell to the floor. Ingrid helpfully picked up the papers and tried to sort them. She jumped when she saw a picture of the two men left on the plane. She read the Interpol announcement. *My God, this quiet old gay couple is wanted for murder!*

Ingrid had a clear, strong feminine voice as she spoke, "Excuse me! Who's in charge here? These men who are wanted for murder are sitting on our plane."

Suddenly, Ingrid had the full attention of all the Port Stanley employees.

"May I see that fax? Why do you have it?" The grey-haired Senior Officer Leonard asked indignantly.

"Pages fell to the floor. I picked them up and recognized the picture."

"I need an armed constable and sergeant to apprehend them."

"I don't think they're armed or dangerous, Officer Leonard," Ingrid said as she watched the policemen put on bulletproof vests and draw their weapons.

"May I remind you they're wanted for murder, Madam?" Officer Leonard sneered.

"Oh. Right," Ingrid replied quietly.

Johnny and Walter were awakened by a stern voice. "Gentlemen, you are under arrest for the murder of Fergus MacCann, known as Amadeus. At our earliest convenience, you will be transported to London." Johnny and Walter looked blearily at the uniformed men with pistols pointed at them.

The Reckoning

On a conference call, Jones and Green cheered to learn that Johnny and Walter were now guests of Port Stanley constabulary in the Falklands. They would travel to Port Stanley to interview the fugitives.

Johnny and Walter were in a cell with a toilet and metal bunk beds built into the stone wall. They sat together on the lower bunk and conversed in whispers. "I'll confess, Walter. You had nothing to do with fiddling the heater that killed Amadeus. You need to go free and live your best life. I'm so sorry to involve you in all this mess."

"I don't regret helping you, luv. Amadeus was an odious man. I'll accept my punishment for helping you stay free for as long as we did. We had a grand time together, didn't we?"

"You've been a wonderful partner, Walter."

"You as well, Johnny."

Their whispered conversation was interrupted by an awakening drunk who started loudly vomiting into a bucket. The smell was of stale beer. It was almost a relief when the constable opened their cell door. "This way, gentlemen. Your British interrogators are here." Each man was placed in a room with a metal table and a large, windowed wall, allowing observers to watch the questioning without being seen. Superintendent Green sat across from Johnny with the tape recorder turned on.

"You've led us on a merry chase, Johnny. We have forensic evidence that reveals you were the one who manipulated the wall heater and closed the window that caused the carbon monoxide death of Fergus MacCann, commonly known as Amadeus. What say you?"

"Amadeus was a horrible person. With his fame and success, he used people and then threw them away. Look at poor Camilla, forced into a botched abortion. I contributed to the arrangements of the early musical albums with no compensation or recognition. I will freely admit I killed Amadeus, but please let Walter go. Walter knew nothing about me jimmying the heater or closing the window. I doubt he understands anything about heaters and the dangers of carbon monoxide."

In an adjacent room, Jones looked at a very tired and aging Walter, sitting nervously across from him. "Walter, why did you assist Johnny in killing Amadeus?"

"Oh, Sir, I would never have assisted in killing Amadeus. I believe Johnny only intended to prank Amadeus with the heater. He was drunk and remembering how Amadeus lorded it over people who had helped make him rich and famous."

"Did you attend the party in the dressing room?"

"Yes, for a short time. I tried to get Johnny to come home with me, but he was drunk and in no mood to leave."

"You realized that the carbon monoxide death of Amadeus was the work of Johnny, didn't you?"

"I had my suspicions. Johnny never told me directly. I'm sure he didn't intend to kill Amadeus, just make him uncomfortable."

"Good try, Walter. You are the one who disposed of the Palladium jacket in Portree. It took some keen shoppers to spot it on the back sale rack."

Walter's mouth was trembling as he spoke. "I knew we had no business with that Palladium jacket. Johnny gets impetuous when he's drunk. Again, I think it was intended as a prank."

"You realized that this hasty attempt to get to Buenos Aires was not for a prank but for a murderer to escape the British authorities."

"I'm an old man who wanted to live out his years with a partner he loved very much. I'm still convinced that Johnny only intended to make Amadeus sick – not kill him."

"Well, Walter, you and Johnny are going to have the opportunity to express your views, but I think you assisted in a murder. We're flying back to London this evening." Jones leaned forward and looked Walter in the eye as he spoke.

Hours later, Green and Jones, plus two burly constables, sat with their prisoners, Johnny and Walter, in business class for a direct flight to London.

When they landed at Heathrow Airport, a waiting transport van drove the prisoners directly to Scotland Yard. A large contingent of reporters and photographers swarmed Johnny and Walter, who walked with handcuffs and shackles. Superintendents Green and Jones, with two days' stubble, spoke with the reporters.

"Johnny MacKay has confessed to the murder of Amadeus. We're charging his partner, Walter, as an accomplice." Superintendent Green stepped back to allow Jones to take the microphone.

"On behalf of Scotland Yard, I want to apologize to both women mistakenly entangled in this murder investigation. They are entirely innocent and will be free to return to America."

Free to Return Home

Thank God they found Amadeus' killer," whispered Prudence and Phyllida as they sighed with relief. They hugged, stood up, and danced around the room where they were watching the evening news on the telly.

"Can we just pack our bags and go?" Prudence looked worried.

"I'm not sure. Let me call the front desk."

"Hello, Sheila, I'm calling to see if Pru and I can just check out now that we are not murder suspects . . . Yes, I'll wait while you confer with the boss." Phyllida was on the speakerphone with Prudence quietly listening.

"It seems we need verification from Superintendent Jones to release your passports. He's expected home to Portree tomorrow or the next day. We're so relieved that you ladies are no longer suspects. We knew you were innocent."

"There's always bureaucracy to deal with. At least our extended stay is paid for by the UK," Phyllida grumbled after hanging up.

"I sure hope that awful reporter, Felicia Friday, stays far, far away from us."

"Let's call our children. It's 10 a.m. in San Francisco!"

"Hello," answered a tired Vanessa. "Are you okay?"

"We're marvelous, darling. They just arrested Johnny MacKay for the murder of Amadeus, and he has confessed."

Prudence held the phone away from her ear as Vanessa shouted for joy.

Phyllida was on the phone with Beth, who burst into tears. "I've been so worried about you, Mother."

The next phone call was for Phyllida from Jones. She put on the speakerphone for Prudence.

"I'll be back day after tomorrow to take you lovely ladies to a special dinner before driving you to the airport in Glasgow for a direct flight to San Francisco."

"Thank you so much, Marcus. What we'd really enjoy is an evening of watching Scottish Country Dancing too. Is that possible?"

"Oh, yes!" Prudence shouted and clapped her hands. "I'll video as much as I can for Vanessa and Yuri."

True to his word, Jones arranged a Scottish Country dance performance with his twin brother, Mattias. Phyllida and Prudence dined on langoustine and Skye Gold beer. After dinner, a room full of dancers with live music danced for two hours on the women's last night in Portree. Marcus and Helen Jones sat with them.

"We struck a plea deal with Johnny MacKay to have Walter under house-arrest at home in Hyde Park. I feel he should have spent jail time for assisting his partner," grumbled Jones as he drained his pint.

"I'm relieved to know who committed the murder and to have Pru and me free of suspicion," Phyllida sighed. "This type of murder speaks of years of resentment boiling over."

The owners of the pub had hung a banner on the wall stating: *Farewell to Beloved American Visitors, Prudence Silver and Phyllida Walker.* The dancers put on an impromptu performance, with the men in MacQueen tartan kilts and the women in black dresses, complete with MacQueen sashes secured to their shoulders with silver brooches. They performed a reel, a jig, a strathspey, and concluded with the Reel of the Royal Scots. Then, two dancers led their American guests out onto the dance floor for a few simple Scottish dances. Jones and his wife joined the set.

"I truly enjoyed this evening. You've made us welcome participants in your culture. It's permanently etched in my memory," Prudence declared.

"I second Pru. Skye will be a host of happy memories." Phyllida toasted the dancers with the last of her Skye Gold.

The following day, Helen and Marcus Jones drove the women three hours to Glasgow. Helen drove most of the way to relieve Marcus, who was still jet-lagged from his whirlwind trip to the Falklands and back.

Their flight to San Francisco was upgraded to business class.

The women enjoyed comfortable seats and slightly better food as they anxiously returned home from a very eventful trip. Phyllida and Prudence gave grandmotherly smiles to a family with three rambunctious children on their way to Disneyland.

Upon their arrival in San Francisco, the U.S. Customs agent said, "Welcome back," as she examined each passport. To her surprise, Prudence answered, "Thank you so much!" as she tucked her passport into her purse. As they stepped into the 4 pm ocean breeze outside the International Terminal at SFO, Yuri was waiting with his father, Mikhail, to drive the women home.

"I'm sure you won't mind knowing that my mother prepared a light supper for you. Vanessa, Beth, and the grandchildren are there to greet you."

"We're honored. Such a lovely thing to do." Phyllida smiled as she saw all the familiar landmarks as they drove from the airport to San Francisco. They drove on Highway 280 to avoid the afternoon traffic jam on Highway 101. At Park Merced, Yuri turned onto Junipero Serra Boulevard. They continued to wind their way through the hilly St. Francis Woods, upper Haight to Masonic and into the Richmond district. All the familiar sights reinforced their safe return.

As they drove up to Yuri's parents' home, everyone dashed to the front yard. Beth, with her nineteen-year-old twins, rushed to hug Phyllida while Vanessa, Ivan, and Dimitry hugged Prudence, who was happy to see that Dimitry and Ivan remembered their grandmother.

Letter to Holly and Milo

Scotland Yard continued the investigation of Johnny MacKay and Walter Watson. The stack of letters and packages they left on the kitchen table of the Hyde Park flat included a letter to Holly. Of course, everything was opened and read. The letter to Holly intrigued Superintendent Green, who called Holly into his office. He handed her an opened letter with the envelope stapled to it. She quietly read.

> *Dear Holly,*
> *Well, darling girl, you are full of surprises. I want you to know that I hold no grudge. You certainly did your job well. I had no idea I was under surveillance. I assure you I still have affection for both you and Milo. If you run into me, rest assured, I am still your friend.*
> *Affectionately, Walter*
> *P.S. Please give Milo an extra treat from me.*

Holly felt tears form as she read this final message from Walter. "Well, Sir, Walter is a sweet and lonely man who enjoyed our conversations at Starbucks."

"Were there any other meetings?" Green leaned forward as he spoke.

"Just the dinner at the Black Swan. That was carefully monitored by our surveillance team."

"I assured top brass that there was no further fraternization between you and Walter. For the time being, I'm assigning you and Milo to the Brighton Beach area. Walter is under house arrest in his Hyde Park apartment. Being out of London will allow you to work without accidentally meeting with Walter. Are you okay with that?"

"Yes, Sir, that would be more comfortable for me."

"Enjoy your reassignment and please give Milo a treat from me as well."

"Thank you. I will."

Holly reached the elevator and used a tissue to dab a stray tear. "Allergies," she stated to her fellow passengers.

As news spread about the international chase of Johnny MacKay and his partner, Walter, Felicia Friday urged her editor to assign her to interview them. Johnny MacKay flatly refused; however, Walter politely agreed to an interview while he was incarcerated. Luckily for him, TAG, Actor's Guild of Great Britain, contacted his agent and began providing financial support. The publicity suddenly had Walter working again, and he was able to retain the flat he previously shared with Johnny MacKay. An ankle monitor allowed Walter to go to work in the London area with permission from his probation officer.

One evening, a few months after moving to Brighton Beach, Holly settled in her rented garden apartment to watch a new mystery series on television. To her amazement, she saw Walter with gleaming white hair and mustache in a teal velvet jacket, introducing the new series. She felt both pleased and sad, remembering chats with him at Starbucks. Milo, curled on his dog bed, perked his ears as he heard Walter. Holly scratched his ears and gave him a dog treat as they watched the telly.

An Evening of Ballet

In the year following their return from Skye, Yuri and Vanessa choreographed a ballet: *Selkie and the Skye Dragon*. Mattias Jones traveled to San Francisco to assist with choreographing Scottish dancing scenes. For the premier performance, the front center rows of the San Francisco War Memorial Opera House were filled with Yuri and Vanessa's family and their Scottish friends, Marcus and Helen Jones, as well as Llewellyn MacCann and her mother, Florence MacCann. Phyllida and Prudence had aisle seats beside Grandma Bella and Grandpa Mikhail.

The ballet opened with a selkie sunning on a rock off the coast of Skye. A large green dragon rose, fiercely undulating, from the sea. As the villagers ran away, a handsome Scotsman, wearing black tights and a MacQueen plaid doublet leaped into the sea to slay the dragon. The Scotsman, danced by Yuri, and the Dragon frantically fought as Yuri continued to attack with many magnificent leaps, his silver sword flashing. As she watched the dragon sink under the water, the selkie shed her gray mantle and appeared as a beautiful maiden with long flowing platinum hair. Vanessa and Yuri danced a pas de deux with sensual lifts and dips. The audience was electrified by the loving chemistry between them. In the final scene, the village danced in a beautiful wedding with Scottish dancing, led by the bride and groom.

As the curtain lowered, loud shouts of "bravo" erupted, followed by a long standing ovation. Yuri and Vanessa bowed for three curtain calls with the cast and conductor. The stage was covered with bouquets tossed on stage by an Opera House volunteer. Yuri and Vanessa took their final bows holding arms full of roses.

Phyllida and Prudence led their guests backstage to congratulate the dancers. They joined the dancers in joyful pandemonium. Finally, they left the cheering dancers so they could change and join family and friends for a late supper at Max's Opera Café.

"Wasn't that simply marvelous!" Phyllida exclaimed as they were seated at Max's.

"It certainly was," cheered Prudence as she took a sip of wine. "Vanessa and Yuri will be joining us shortly; they just texted."

Phyllida suddenly turned to Prudence to whisper, "My God, I think that's Felicia Friday with some man in the booth across the room."

As Prudence looked over, Felicia Friday pulled up the hood of her black trench coat.

Everyone at the table cheered as Yuri and Vanessa joined them. Before sitting, Yuri and Vanessa walked around the table, giving each person a squeeze on the shoulder and a red rose. "Both love and sadness in our recent Scottish experiences created this ballet. Thanks to you, love overcame sadness."

As the dancers took their seats, a whisper around the table pointed out Felicia Friday and her friend at a nearby booth. Superintendent Jones spoke quietly, "I'm away from my jurisdiction, but that woman needs to be put on notice and shamed for her harmful articles that subjected Prudence and Phyllida to being detained as murder suspects."

Everyone at the table stood and surrounded the booth. Friday looked up with a quivering mouth and wide eyes.

"Your irresponsibly suggestive articles put these lovely ladies under suspicion as murderers. Scotland Yard's investigation of Amadeus' murder was slowed and hampered by your innuendos." Superintendent Jones spoke in a low threatening voice as he continued, "There had better not be any further attempts at sensational articles involving innocent people. Scotland Yard takes considerable umbrage at having to disprove your outlandish suggestions and we know who you are by reputation."

Suddenly, Felicia's face brightened with a broad smile. "I was really here to attend this ballet and write a review with my fiancé, Josh. He's also my editor. It was wonderful, by the way. I'm truly sorry about the problems caused by my article involving Prudence Silver and Phyllida Walker, and I'm so relieved that you found the murderer. I would love to schedule an interview with the two ballet stars, Yuri and Vanessa. Maybe I could do an article about Prudence and Phyllida with an update of where they are now?"

"Get in touch with the San Francisco Ballet press agent but leave Prudence and Phyllida alone," Yuri growled.

As they returned to their table, food arrived. After the ballet and excitement, everyone had a hearty appetite and eagerly shared extra orders of latkes with applesauce and sour cream and mini Reuben sandwiches. There was a quiet lull while everyone ordered coffee and waited for dessert.

Yuri rose and walked over to the piano player who had just begun playing. He put $20 in the tip jar with a special request. As "I Could Have Danced All Night" began, Yuri formally bowed to Vanessa with an invitation to dance. The couple waltzed around the room with many twirls. At the end of their waltz, Yuri twirled Vanessa to his left, then right for formal curtsies. The room erupted in applause from both patrons and wait staff.

Two waiters placed a giant strawberry shortcake, adorned with sparklers in the middle of the table to further applause and cheers. In the quiet as everyone finished, Llewellyn MacCann and her mother, Florence stood, flanked by Marcus and Mattias Jones.

A clink on a glass brought the table to attention. Llewellyn took a deep breath, then began speaking. "We have been on a long sad journey following the death of my father, Amadeus. My mother and brothers have agreed to plan a memorial for Amadeus on his birthday this coming spring. We will invite Vanessa, Yuri, Prudence, and Phyllida to attend and participate. We hope to share memories of Amadeus' convoluted life and work that will make all of us smile and love him for the unique and talented man he was."

After a stunned silence, the table applauded.

"Amadeus would love it!" exclaimed Prudence. "Philly and I will be there."

"Yuri and I will attend as well," Vanessa spoke through tears.

Yuri stood. "This is a special conclusion to this magical evening as a gift to all friends and family present."

After dessert, two musicians from an adjacent table rose with bagpipes to play the "Skye Boatman's Song." Friends and family danced out of the room into a soft mist of fog in San Francisco.

About the Author

*L*ast Song on Skye is T.E. Swan's debut novel, the first in a series. In this superbly woven plot, she blends her investigative experience with her love of mystery novels featuring wise women.

With a bacteriology degree from the University of Tennessee, Knoxville, Ms. Swan became the first woman investigator in the U.S. Food and Drug Administration, where she worked as a field investigator in an all-male environment. She recalls when a worker at a manufacturing site pointed to her as she stood in the investigative team, and asked, "Who's that woman?" The response was, "That's no woman. She's an FDA Inspector." Eight years later, she transferred to the newly established U.S. Consumer Product Safety Administration (CPSC). While working there, she earned her M.S. in Environmental Science from the University of San Francisco. At CPSC, Ms. Swan collaborated with law enforcement agencies in investigations involving suspected criminal activity.

T.E. Swan thanks OLLI San Francisco State and her writing instructor, Diane Frank, for encouraging and honing her writing skills. She lives in San Francisco with her family near Lafayette Park.